# In Search of Shipki La

# In Search of Shipki La

John Pollard

| | | |
|---|---|---|
| Library of Congress Control Number: | | 2013917374 |
| ISBN: | Hardcover | 978-1-4931-3476-2 |
| | Softcover | 978-1-4931-0573-1 |
| | eBook | 978-1-4931-0575-5 |

Rev. date: 02/11/2014

**To order additional copies of this book, contact:**
Xlibris LLC
1-800-455-039
www.Xlibris.com.au
Orders@Xlibris.com.au
520580

# CONTENTS

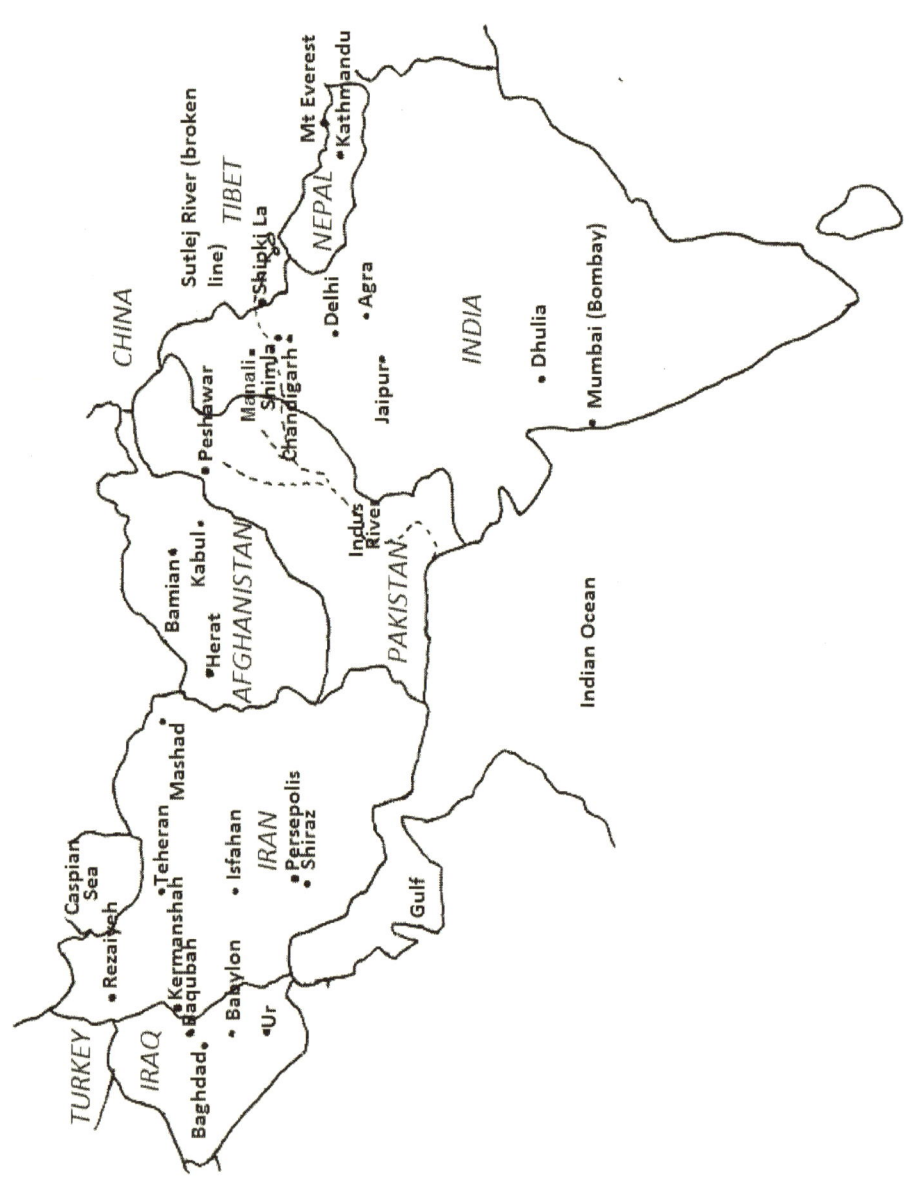

Afghanistan and neighbouring countries.

# 1

# Mysterious Disappearance

IT WAS A normal Wednesday morning. Hugh and Ruth woke to the 7:00 a.m. radio news and classical music and enjoyed a relaxed breakfast downstairs. After completing some essential household chores, they sat outside with their young black Labrador to drink a mid-morning coffee and enjoy the late summer sunshine. It was still a great joy and novelty for Hugh, who had retired nine months earlier, that he no longer had to fight the daily peak-hour traffic on the way to work. When they had finished the coffee and given the dog a few small things to eat, Ruth drove to the local supermarket to do some household shopping for the remainder of the week whilst Hugh sat down with the financial section of the *Sydney Morning Herald.*

The peaceful atmosphere was broken by the sound of the postman's small motor bike. 'He's early today' flashed through Hugh's mind as he got up and walked to the gate. There must have been quite a lot of mail for the neighbouring houses, because the mailman only reached the gate at the same time as Hugh, and the two exchanged a few pleasantries and remarks about the weather. There was a pile of mail for them too, and Hugh thumbed through the envelopes as he strolled back to the house.

Most of the mail was routine—bills to pay, bank statements, and charity donation requests. A more formal-looking priority letter from the USA caught his eye, and he opened it as soon as he sat down inside. The letterhead revealed that it came from Buffalo Investigations and Forensic Inc., located in Buffalo, New York State. Below the letterhead, the company claimed 'more than 50 years' experience in corporate, marital, legal support, missing persons, IT forensics, bug detection, polygraph, and workplace theft'. Hugh was intrigued and immediately read the letter that was dated 5 March 2003.

*Dear Mr Webster,*

*I am writing in the hope that you may be able to help us in relation to the case of the missing son of an elderly widow who disappeared 35 years ago in the latter part of 1968 or early 1969. Our company handled the initial investigations, but was forced to put the case aside after a couple of years due to a lack of any useful new leads.*

*As I said above, our client is an elderly widow and she is anxious to discover the fate of her son before she dies.*

*There is strong evidence that he disappeared in Afghanistan or one of the neighbouring countries. She has recently learned from a friend in Australia that you were in this region about that time, and the information we have from our early investigations indicated that the missing son was in contact with some unnamed Australians in Afghanistan and possibly elsewhere. Other details we have suggest that you may very well be able to assist us in solving this mysterious case and provide closure for this lady.*

*There is much more information I can disclose if you agree to meet me. I sincerely hope you will.*

*I can be contacted at the above address. Because there is some need for haste in this matter, I would prefer it if you either e-mailed me your response or telephoned me (reversing charges, of course). In the event that you agree to assist us, I shall fly to Sydney immediately to fill you in with all the details of the case and seek relevant information from you. Our client is a woman of considerable means and you can be assured that any costs you incur will be promptly reimbursed.*

*Sincerely,*
*Andy McInnis*

Hugh read the letter several times and then leaned back in his chair trying to recall the people he and Ruth had met thirty-five years earlier during their 1968 journey.

Ruth returned in time for lunch. As soon as she arrived, he showed her the letter and they discussed it over the meal. Like Hugh, she was intrigued. The letter seemed genuine. Should they get involved? Were there any risks? Would they be putting themselves in any danger if there had been foul play? Would the whole thing simply be a nuisance and waste of time? Should they try to help this elderly woman? Anyway, what possible help could they provide?

They decided to mull the issues over for a day or so before e-mailing their answer.

# 2

# 35 Years Earlier

THAT EVENING, HUGH got out their ancient slide projector, and they enjoyed a couple of hours of nostalgia looking through the hundreds of pictures of their three-month adventure in 1968 driving from Wales to India. Years had passed since they last looked at them, and they were delighted that the colours were still as clear as the day they received them back from the developers.

Conscious that there might be a photograph of someone relevant to the missing person case, they particularly looked carefully at anyone appearing in their slides.

The only people in the slides for the United Kingdom and Europe were family and friends. In Turkey, Iraq, and Iran, the only persons, apart from themselves, were local people. It was only in Afghanistan that other Western travellers appeared, and these were few and far between.

The first such slide was a group photograph taken somewhere between the Iran-Afghanistan border and Herat. Hugh and Ruth had met the other travellers at the border and agreed to pitch camp off the road somewhere before Herat. They recalled the evening well. There were three vehicles: a Citroen belonging to a Swiss couple, Inge and Patrick; a VW bug belonging to two printers, Gavyn and Dai, from Abergavenny in Wales; and their own Mini Traveller. The party of six stopped as evening approached and set up camp, electing to sleep under the stars. None of their camping companions seemed likely candidates either as the missing man, presumably American, or a friend of his, or an assassin—if indeed the missing man had been murdered.

They remembered relaxing and preparing their evening meal. It was just getting dark when about a dozen wild-looking Afghan men suddenly appeared and selected a small knoll close to the travellers' camp to pray facing Mecca. Talk at the camp suddenly became a little strained. The fact that many of the Afghanis seemed more interested in observing the campers than attending to their prayers was, to say the least, a little unnerving. None of the travellers carried weapons, and the locals were all conspicuously well armed. Eventually the locals departed and night fell. As soon as they were out of sight, conversation became more animated, but it was clear that they all felt a little frightened. The tension gradually eased, and they all chuckled when Gavyn revealed that he was carrying several large fireworks that he would ignite to frighten off any uninvited person who might creep up on them in the dark. No one felt reassured!

Nevertheless, they all eventually fell asleep under the stars. In the morning, as he was struggling out of his sleeping bag, Hugh was startled to discover a large scorpion on the edge of the bag. It was the first he had ever seen. He had been about to brush it off with his bare hand, thinking it was a small twig, and was very relieved that he did not do so!

The pictures at the campsite certainly brought back memories.

The next couple of slides featuring non-local people were taken in Kabul at the official tourist campsite a few days later. One showed the group who had camped together near Herat. The second, in less-than-perfect focus, showed three young men, two in semi-local attire, all bearded and of hippy appearance. Neither Hugh nor Ruth could recall their names, if indeed they ever knew them, and they could not recall as to why they had taken the photograph. Perhaps it was their appearance.

After several days in the capital, Hugh and Ruth had set out for Bamian, famous for its two huge Buddhas carved into the cliffs above the village. Patrick and Inge joined them in their Citroen. For the first one hundred kilometres north, the road was good, and they made rapid progress. They then turned west towards the interior on an abominable road, which in places was little more than a rough track. Night fell, and they camped above three thousand metres in the Hindu Kush mountains. It was bitterly cold, and for warmth, the four travellers shared a small inflatable tent belonging to the Swiss couple. Unfortunately one of the three upright tubes had a small leak, and Patrick had to leave the tent several times during the night to pump it up.

Although there were four of them in the confined space, they were still freezing cold and got up as soon as the sun appeared over the mountain peaks. A few hours later and after a couple of encounters with stone-throwing boys, they reached the Buddhas, which were even more impressive than their depiction in the Afghan tourist literature. On the return journey to Kabul, they passed an abandoned 'ugly duckling' Citroen, which had been accidentally driven into an enormous crater in the middle of a collapsed bridge. There seemed to be an Afghan guarding it, although they did not communicate with him. They had felt very sorry for the vehicle owner, who had driven the car into the country and would not be able to take it out again. The owner might even have to pay import duty on the car—unless the Afghan authorities were convinced it was a complete write-off.

The rough road to and from Bamian had placed a big toll on Hugh and Ruth's Mini: its starter motor had burnt out and a couple of the engine mountings had broken. There was nowhere in Kabul to have these defects repaired. Fortunately the car could be driven, with care, but they had to nurse it along and roll-start it every time the engine was turned off.

It was clear from their visits to the Kabul markets that Western travellers were not welcome in the country—at least as far as some of the locals were concerned. Each time they returned to camp from public places, they found unpleasant wet patches on the back of their clothing where people had spat on them. Patrick and Inge had thoroughly enjoyed the detour to Bamian and had purchased a large earthenware water jug for Hugh and Ruth as a 'thank you' gift. The Websters still had the jug outside at the front of their house in Sydney.

They were due to continue on their way to Pakistan and India a few days later. Given the condition of the car and a warning from the Afghan government that it could not guarantee the safety of anyone remaining in the Khyber Pass after dusk, they were pleased when an Australian couple, Ken and Janet, from Adelaide, who were camped nearby, announced that they too would drive through into Pakistan the same day. The two couples agreed to meet up from time to time en route. Ken and Janet were driving a VW Kombi and, as it turned out, would share much of the next few weeks with Hugh and Ruth, into the Himalayan foothills and then on to Delhi, Agra, Jaipur, and finally, Bombay. Hugh and Ruth had several photographs of these travelling companions, but they doubted they had anything to do with the missing man.

Having reviewed all their photographs of the three-month journey, it seemed that there was nothing they could contribute to the puzzle of the missing man. What should they do?

It seemed that there was nothing they could contribute. Then they remembered Hugh's detailed diary/log, which detailed each day of their journey. So they scanned through its pages the next morning.

In European and western Turkey, they had met a few overland travellers, but as far as they could see, none seemed relevant to the case.

Further on, in south-eastern Turkey, Iraq, and western Iran, they had encountered no other foreign travellers.

The diary did record a few interesting people they had encountered at the official and relatively comfortable campsite on the western edge of Teheran, aptly named 'The Oasis'. Hugh and Ruth had used this campsite as their base for a few days as they explored the Iranian capital. The site had a high mud wall around it and the luxury of a swimming pool. Most overland travellers found it a convenient place to stay before continuing their dusty overland journey east or west.

The campers mentioned in the diary included six grandmothers driving two Land Rovers from England to Australia. They were not mechanically-minded and seem to have had their lack of knowledge exploited by unscrupulous mechanics along the way. There were also two young British women en route to Australia, who had met in New York and decided to see the world by car together. They had driven across the USA and down to the tip of South America, shipped their car to South Africa, and then driven home to Scotland to see their folks. By comparison, Hugh and Ruth had felt like 'Sunday drivers'. The only others mentioned in the diary were two lean young Americans on their way to Afghanistan. It seemed that they wandered fairly freely between Turkey and Afghanistan. Hugh and Ruth had no photographs of any of these travellers and no record of their names. One or both of the Americans could perhaps be of interest, but it seemed a remote chance.

They continued reading through the diary record of their 1968 adventure, indulging themselves in the nostalgia the account brought them. The first major city after Kabul and the Khyber Pass was Peshawar. They had been somewhat surprised but delighted to find that there was a British Motor Corporation approved motor centre there, and they had left the Mini at the workshop to have its numerous problems rectified. After Afghanistan and the remoter parts of Iran, the discovery of the well-equipped centre had given them the impression that they were back in civilization. As soon as they started wandering around town, however, they quickly discovered that Peshawar was in fact a very wild frontier city, where one could change money on the black market at very favourable rates and purchase all types of black market goods—watches, gems, jewellery, cameras, cars, genuine and replica guns of all types, and other weapons. Even so, they did not feel particularly threatened as they wandered around the city, waiting for the car to be repaired. Thinking back thirty-five years later and with the benefit of knowing what had subsequently occurred in Afghanistan and Pakistan, they realised they were probably naïve.

As they recalled the day in Peshawar, Ruth suddenly remembered something not recorded in Hugh's diary: Ken and Janet had picked up a bearded young man in Peshawar, who then travelled with them for some days, but kept very much to himself. He might have been one of the Americans in their Kabul campsite photograph, but after so many years, their memory of him was vague. They recalled, however, that he stayed out of sight most of the time, and on the couple of occasions they were actually in his company, he was reluctant to engage in conversation. He seemed to disappear at night as they continued on their journey across Pakistan and into India. For some reason, Ken and Janet had been reluctant to talk about their passenger.

Ruth and Hugh tried to recollect all that they had observed relating to the mystery man.

'I think he was a source of irritation between Ken and Janet and that is why they did not want to discuss him with us. It would lead to an argument between them,' was Ruth's suggestion.

'I think you may be right,' was her husband's response. 'I seem to recall that Janet appeared to feel sorry for him and that Ken did not really want him travelling with them.'

Hugh and Ruth did not see him again after Rampur in the Himalayan foothills, and he had certainly disappeared by the time they reached Delhi. They had surmised that he was probably a US draft dodger who smoked pot, but that was only a guess. At the Indian border, he had seemed to have had a little difficulty with the authorities, at least initially, but after disappearing into the immigration/customs office for a short time, he had reappeared and continued travelling with Ken and Janet.

No other Western tourists or overland travellers were featured in the diary or their memories of the remainder of their journey to Bombay.

The question remained: What answer should they give the private investigator? There were also associated questions. Would the little information they had about a few people they had met in Iran, Afghanistan, Pakistan, and India thirty-five years earlier be of any use? Would the grieving mother gain any solace from any information they could provide? If there had been foul play, and they cooperated in the investigation, would they be placing themselves in any danger?

Perhaps they should find out more about Buffalo Investigations and Forensic Inc. before making their decision. So they googled the company and found a number of links. The company's home page revealed that it was established in 1947 and described the types of work it performed and the help it could provide clients. It emphasised the international contacts it had and outlined the experience of its senior staff. There were also links to newspaper articles where the company's name was mentioned. None of these suggested any impropriety in the investigator's activities. Finally, there was a short newspaper article that reviewed and compared the larger private investigator companies in the north-east USA. Buffalo came out reasonably well.

Hugh and Ruth had four adult children and a granddaughter, and the thought of the grieving mother eventually persuaded them. They would reveal what little information they had and leave it at that. So they e-mailed the following letter to the agent.

*Dear Mr McInnis,*

*We doubt that we can be of much help in this matter. We have looked back through our photographs of this period and also checked our diary/log record of the journey. The only things that have a remote chance of being relevant to your investigation are the following:*

1. *We have a few photographs of people we met and/or travelled with in Afghanistan and neighbouring countries. None of these appears to us to be relevant to the case, except perhaps a slightly fuzzy photograph of three unshaven young men in semi-Afghan attire who were at the hill campsite in Kabul.*

2. *Our diary record mentions two 'lean young American men' who seemed to travel back and forth in the Turkey/Iran/Afghanistan region, whom we encountered only very briefly at the Teheran campsite. We do not have photographs of them or any other record of our casual encounter, and no names.*

3. *From Kabul to Bombay (Mumbai), we travelled in convoy with another Australian couple, who, we seem to recall, carried a passenger with them for part of the time. We think he was American. We have no photographs of him, nor any diary record, which is strange. He did keep very much to himself, and our recollection is that he ceased travelling with the other couple near Rampur in the Himalayan foothills east of Shimla.*

*We are sorry that we can be of such little help, and only hope that in providing this information we help in your reopened investigation and that eventually it brings some solace to your client.*

JOHN POLLARD

*Yours sincerely,*
*Hugh and Ruth Webster*

Within twenty-four hours, they had an e-mail response from the investigator.

*Dear Hugh and Ruth,*
*Thank you very much for the information you have provided. I believe that some of it is worth following up. I shall therefore contact my client and seek her permission to reveal her identity and provide the information we already have from our early investigations. With her agreement, I will then organise a flight to Sydney to meet you (assuming that you are agreeable to meet me).*

*Andy McInnis*

So much for providing a little information and leaving it at that! Still, meeting Andy McInnis in Sydney would not really be a problem or commit them in any way to the ongoing investigation, and by now they were becoming somewhat intrigued by the mystery and wanted to know more. They e-mailed their agreement.

Andy's follow-up e-mail came two days later.

*Dear Hugh and Ruth,*
*My client has seen the information you kindly provided and has agreed to me meeting you in Sydney and providing you with all the relevant information we have. She is keen that I quiz you about your time in the region and the people you met. In fact, she has instructed me to do so. I hope this will be okay with you.*
*I have booked a flight arriving Sydney on Tuesday, 25 March, and will be staying in the Wentworth Hotel in the city centre. Do you know it?*
*Would it be possible for you to meet me there on Wednesday 26? I have your telephone number and will call you on my arrival to arrange the time and other details.*
*Would you please be kind enough to e-mail me your agreement to meet and your availability that week?*

*Andy*

They e-mailed their agreement and confirmed their availability.

# 3

# Memories

OVER THE NEXT week, the case was seldom far from Hugh and Ruth's thoughts, and they mused as to what Andy McInnis would be like and what they might learn when they met him. Tuesday evening around 7:00 p.m., they received a call from him. Ruth took the call and was surprised to hear a strong Scottish accent. They spoke for only a few minutes and arranged to meet at the Wentworth Hotel the next day at 10:00 a.m. They had already set aside the whole day for their discussions.

Hugh and Ruth took the train to Wynyard Station and walked to the Wentworth Hotel, arriving a few minutes before 10:00 a.m. At the reception desk, Hugh asked to speak with Mr Andy McInnis on the house phone. Andy came on line and indicated that he would be down immediately.

The couple's first reaction when he approached was that he was tall, athletic and muscular, and younger than they had imagined. He greeted them with a friendly smile and a firm handshake. After a few minutes' polite chatter and enquiries about his flight, they took the lift upstairs to a small conference room the private investigator had booked. Andy ordered coffee, and while they waited, the 'getting-to-know-you' conversation continued.

Hugh judged Andy to be around 40 years of age, and it was clear therefore that he could not have been involved in the original investigation. As their conversation continued, they learned he had only been with Buffalo Investigations and Forensic Inc. two years. Before that, he was employed briefly with a small private investigation company in Glasgow after two years with the police. He moved to the USA following his divorce in 2001.

Andy poured the coffee and told them that he had quite a lot of information relating to the missing man, which he promised to reveal in its entirety in due course. Before doing so, however, he wanted to hear their story, in case what he told them subconsciously affected their personal account.

He took out a notepad and pencil as the couple began their story.

They explained that after marrying in 1967, they had spent a year at the University of Chicago, where they carefully planned the overland journey that would take Hugh back home to Sydney and Ruth to her new home. They had set out from Ruth's home city Cardiff in a heavily laden Morris Mini Traveller with sufficient basic food and medical supplies for three months on the road as well as three spare tyres, two of which were placed under Ruth's feet inside the car. As they traversed the UK and Europe, they had called in to say goodbye to family and friends in Dorset, the Netherlands, Belgium, and Switzerland before crossing Italy, Yugoslavia, Bulgaria, and Greece, and entering Turkey not far from Edirne. It was here that they first heard the call to prayer from a minaret and their real overland journey began. At night their car radio picked up stations from many different countries in a variety of languages. The Soviet Union call tune 'Midnight in Moscow' came through loud and clear, most likely from somewhere in the Ukraine.

After spending a few days exploring Istanbul, they took the ferry across the Bosphorus to Asiatic Turkey. 'There was no bridge in those days,' Hugh explained. Travelling first to Bursa, they then drove over to the west coast at Canakkale, where they looked across the narrow waterway separating them from the Gallipoli peninsula. Time unfortunately prevented them visiting the WWI campaign area that Hugh had toured two years earlier with two Cambridge friends. At that time, there were no tourists at all.

What delighted them both now on their overland journey was the almost complete absence of tourists at the ancient sites they were now visiting at Troy, Pergamum, Izmir, and Ephesus. There were good but little utilised campsites attached to certain BP service stations, and they took advantage of the comfort and security these provided. They were also inexpensive. There were few other people staying in the campsites, and all of them were visitors from Europe—mainly French. Hugh and Ruth were the only travellers in the area taking the long overland route to India. Other overlanders tended to take the direct route across Turkey through Ankara.

Andy was becoming enthralled by the way in which his new acquaintances recalled with enthusiasm the memories of their travels thirty-five years earlier when he would have been only a child. But he also had a job to do and asked whether by this stage they had in fact met any overlanders. As far as Hugh and Ruth could remember, the only ones were a Pakistani family en route to the United Kingdom, where they hoped to settle. They had met them in European Turkey, at the BP campsite in Edirne, or maybe it was Istanbul—they could not recall which. They could not remember any others, although there were probably some they had not met staying in the campsites of European Turkey.

In Izmir, they managed to purchase a new tyre to replace one that was irreparably damaged on a rough road further north near Ephesus, where they were the only tourists in the famous ancient city. From here, they had turned inland through hot dry countryside over unsurfaced roads to Pammukkale, famous for its hot springs and 'stone waterfalls' formed from the chemicals in the water. There was no formal campsite, and they had camped out a couple of metres from a deep pond of warm spring water. They had swum in it before bed. Andy asked again about other travellers, and once again, all Hugh and Ruth could remember was a small number of European campers on holiday, but no one travelling overland.

The next day, they had wandered around the neighbouring ancient ruined city of Hierapolis and marvelled at a building from at least Roman times with a huge stone arch roof still standing after two millennia despite the numerous earthquakes to which the region is subject. The large 'city of the dead' below the ancient living city also fascinated them. From Konya (ancient Iconium), their route took them through Yesihisar to Urgup and Goreme in Cappadocia to admire the underground houses and churches, where Christians had lived more than a thousand years earlier.

Hugh anticipated Andy's now standard question and remarked, 'No, Andy, on this part of the journey, we neither saw nor met any overland travellers. Nor did we see or meet any as we continued east to Tetvan on the south-west tip of Lake Van and proceeded east along the southern coast of that large salt lake to Van. As I said earlier, I believe almost all overland travellers at that time took the much more direct route further north through Ankara.'

Andy had visited none of these places and was evidently becoming more and more interested in the story the Australians were telling. Whilst what they were telling him about this part of their journey did not seem directly relevant to his investigation, he encouraged them to continue. Ruth surmised that the detail they were able to provide indicated to him that their whole story was indeed credible and any information they might provide would be reliable.

'Do you want me to continue with the details of this part of our journey?' Hugh asked. 'Yes, please,' was the answer. So he continued.

'Our memories of the south-east corner of Turkey include the dusty and sometimes difficult dirt roads, the remoteness of the region, camping at a military post beside the bridge over the Euphrates River, little boys throwing rocks at our car from cliffs above us—great fun for them but a worry for us, the car becoming covered from window level down with wet tar on the outskirts of Van, Ruth's panties being stolen overnight from the clothesline we erected whilst camped in the grounds of the Van police station, a remote ruined castle, and some friendly, hospitable Kurdish nomads. No tourists. We entered Iran on the CENTO military road.

'We were still completely on our own as we drove south from Rezaiyeh in Iran to Kermanshah and then west into Iraq. Our first night was in a very simple hotel with very little privacy in Baqubah, about sixty kilometres east of Baghdad. A smartly dressed Kurdish man in a Western suit and tie found it for us and, as we discovered later, had prepaid the cost. We remember him well, because a week later, after driving south from Baghdad through the scorching desert to Babylon and Ur and back, we were invited to stay in his family home. We were both suffering from heat exhaustion and not well, still recovering from temperatures of 102 degrees Fahrenheit. As a guest in his house, I felt constrained to accept his invitation to go with him to his club—despite my poor health and an infected eye. At the club, he must have drugged my beer, because when I was soundly asleep in bed that night, he tried to seduce Ruth who was sleeping in a single bed on the other side of the room! All the other Iraqi inhabitants we met were friendly and helpful. He was just too friendly!

'I guess the most memorable events in Iraq—apart from the attempted seduction!—were the glories of Babylon, swimming in the Euphrates near that city, the huge lonely Ziggurat towering over the ruins of ancient Ur with nothing but scorching desert around it for hundreds of miles in all directions, and the very kind Iraqis who helped us when we broke down and were stranded in the desert. I think we were very fortunate to visit the four-thousand-year-old ziggurat when we did. A colleague saw it a year or so later and told me that a huge power station had been constructed not far away, and I understand that Saddam

Hussein had the structure partially reconstructed. I suspect that it would have received damage during the recent wars and unrest.'

'Iraq is very much in the news these days. Tell me more about these Iraqis please.'

'Well, we left El Nasiriyah near Ur at 5:00 a.m. to avoid the heat of the day. Unfortunately, our early start failed to prevent us experiencing the full heat of the desert, because a couple of hours into the journey, we incurred a flat tyre followed by a second. We sat in the car for a while wondering what to do and fearing what the increasing temperature might do to our bodies already affected by heat exhaustion.

'We were there for about half an hour when dust rising in the distance heralded an approaching vehicle. It turned out to be a bus. When it stopped, a dozen Arabs in flowing robes clambered out and asked what the problem was. They spoke Arabic, but it was easy to understand what they were asking and easy to show them the problem The bus driver offered to take the two wheels for repairs in the next town about fifty miles away—I forget its name. We were hesitant about doing this—being left with a three-wheel car in the hot desert, but soon decided that we had no alternative. So there we were stranded in the desert with a disabled car.

'We waited a few hours, becoming hotter and hotter as the sun rose higher and more and more anxious, fearing that we would never see our wheels again. Some dust rising in the distance turned out not to be a mirage. It was the bus returning. Out climbed the driver and a different group of Arabs. The driver proudly showed us one repaired tyre, but the other was beyond repair. The onlookers then insisted on helping to put the missing wheel back on the car. And the cost—about five shillings! The Iraqis were wonderful.

'It was only in recent times that we learned that this was the first year of Saddam Hussein's reign of terror.

'We were still off the usual overland route as we returned to Iran from Baqubah and headed south from Kermanshah and Hamadan to ancient Persepolis and Shiraz. The only tourists we met were two German women at the hotel near Persepolis, but I don't think they were travelling overland.'

Andy was intrigued. 'You mentioned Persepolis. I seem to recall that there were big celebrations there many years ago in the time of the Shah. I think royals and world leaders gathered there to celebrate two thousand years of the Persian empire or some such thing.'

'That's a long time ago. You must have been young then!'

'Aye.'

'Persepolis must have been simply amazing before Alexander the Great burned and destroyed it and killed most of its inhabitants. Like all the other sites we visited in Turkey and beyond, the ruined city was not fenced off and there was no entry fee. We spent some time there during the day admiring the building ruins, particularly the extensive bas-relief figures on the stairs and elsewhere, and we returned for another visit in the cool of the evening. We drove a few miles away to the nearby huge royal tombs carved into the cliff face to eat our evening meal and did the same in the morning for breakfast.

'I'd better stop reminiscing and get back to matters possibly more directly relevant to the case!

'It was only when we arrived on the outskirts of Teheran that we found ourselves back on the usual overland route. As we said in our e-mail, we encountered quite a few overland travellers at The Oasis campsite on the western outskirts of Teheran. I think we mentioned the grandmothers, the Scottish girls, and two skinny Americans. Re-reading my diary, we found a reference to some other travellers: five young men, students at Edinburgh University, who were on their way home after a geological survey in the Hindu Kush mountains north-east of Kabul. I don't have their names and I doubt they would have any connection with your enquiry.'

'Are you certain you have no names or photographs of any of these people?'

'Yes. We've checked several times.

'After Teheran, we headed north and east to Gonbad-e-Gaboos and the Caspian Sea, where we were chased out of town by an angry mob of stone-throwing youths. We don't know why they did this, but it was rather frightening. There were just the two of us. The road east was stony and dusty. We saw no other overlanders until the other side of Mashad in far north-eastern Iran, not far from the Afghan border.

'I can't remember whether we mentioned these travellers to you in our e-mail: two printers, Gavyn and Dai, from Aberystwyth, Wales, and a Swiss couple, Patrick and Inge. We camped with them between the border and Herat. As the sun set, we attracted the attention of about a dozen very wild-looking, armed Afghan men, who knelt on a knoll close by to pray, facing Mecca. Although we all felt rather uneasy, we still slept out in the open under the stars.

'Fortunately, we were undisturbed. When we woke up the next morning, I found a scorpion on my sleeping bag!

'We're certain our companions were ordinary overland travellers like ourselves, seeking adventure. We also camped near them in Kabul and travelled north for a few days to Bamian with Inge and Patrick to admire the famous enormous Buddhas carved into the cliff face, but sadly destroyed by the Taliban a couple of years ago—vandalism that almost brings tears to my eyes whenever I think about it.'

'That's interesting,' interrupted Andy. 'I've read about their destruction, but of course haven't seen them. What were they like to visit?'

'The very difficult detour to Bamian was certainly worth it. Once again we were the only tourists there. The taller Buddha stood about 175 feet high and visitors around AD 700 reported both Buddhas being covered with gold and jewels. When we were there, we were free to wander around and climb near the feet of the larger one, but there was no gold or jewels! They were simply huge figures carved into the sandstone cliff.'

'Thanks. I envy you having seen them.'

'After Kabul, we didn't see Inge and Patrick again. They were staying a few days longer in the Afghan capital. I think they were planning to drive on to Nepal—but that is only a very hazy recollection. We ran into the two printers, Gavyn and Dai, again quite by chance much later at the docks in Bombay, where they were trying to ship their vehicle to New Zealand where they planned to work.'

It was almost 1:00 p.m., and after a brief discussion, they decided to stay put and order a light sandwich meal, which arrived promptly, and they ate without talking very much.

After lunch, Hugh continued to recount the story of their journey. He referred to the various people who were camped at the Kabul campsite when they were there. The only ones they could recall were those in their photographs: the Welsh lads, the Swiss couple, and three bearded young men in semi-local attire in a rather fuzzy photograph. At this stage, Andy who had been listening carefully to their story and had been taking notes became very attentive.

'Do you recall the names of any of these young men?'

'No. I don't think we really met them. I think I took the photograph surreptitiously because I was interested in the way they were dressed.'

'Do you know what they were doing in Kabul?'

'No. Our impression at the time was that they were hippies and possibly draft dodgers from the Vietnam War.'

'Do you know how long they were staying there in Kabul?'

'No idea. They seemed to be more or less semi-permanent residents. I had the impression that they moved around a little in Afghanistan and possibly elsewhere—but that was just an impression.'

'Were any of them the same as those you reported meeting briefly in Teheran?'

'They may have been. I'm not sure. The ones in Teheran were also somewhat scruffy, but wore Western clothes. Our encounter in Teheran was only very brief, and we had virtually no contact with the three in Kabul. I'm sorry I can't be more precise.'

Ruth confirmed what Hugh had said.

Andy took detailed notes of Hugh's answers to each of these questions. When he had finished writing, he urged them to continue their story.

Hugh explained that after the journey to Bamian, their car was in a very bad state. The engine mountings had broken and the starter motor had burned out. They had to roll-start the car. There was nowhere in Kabul where they could get the car repaired, but they hoped to find a suitable place in Pakistan. Because of the state of their car and the fact that the Afghan government clearly stated in the documents they carried that it could not guarantee the safety of anyone in the Khyber Pass after 6:00 p.m., they were a little anxious about the onward journey. They were pleased, therefore, to meet an Australian couple from Adelaide travelling in a VW Kombi wagon who wanted to head south at the same time. They agreed to meet up frequently during the journey and make sure Hugh and Ruth got through the famous pass safely.

Andy, clearly vitally interested, interrupted, 'You mentioned them in your e-mail. What were their names?'

'Ken and Janet.'

'Surname?'

'Sorry. We don't have a record of that in our diary. There's a remote chance that we have it written down somewhere on one of the many miscellaneous documents we retained as souvenirs from the journey, but it's a remote chance.'

Andy made some notes and then asked them to continue.

'We got through the pass okay and into Pakistan and stayed in a cheap hostel before Peshawar. We were very relieved the next morning to discover a British Motor Corporation workshop in Peshawar, and we left the car there for a day for repairs. This gave us plenty of time to explore the city. The people were not unfriendly, but it certainly was a wild town, with black market operators offering generous exchange rates for foreign currency; shops selling black market watches, jewellery, and cars; and numerous other shops selling replica and genuine guns of all types as well as other weapons. It was a real Wild West!

'We continued travelling with Ken and Janet. I think we all felt more secure travelling together, and they were interested in the side journey we planned to take to Shimla and Shipki La on the Tibetan border. We mentioned in our e-mail that Ken and Janet had a passenger with them after Peshawar. He kept very much hidden. For some reason, he always disappeared when we stopped for the night in Pakistan and India and reappeared in the morning. Ken and Janet told us that they thought he was a draft dodger. He was very furtive and nervous, and they had the impression he feared being apprehended by US authorities. To us this seemed rather implausible in Pakistan and India, but Ken and Janet seemed convinced. All the time he was with them, they seemed a little on edge, and we wondered why they allowed him to continue travelling with them, particularly given his unusual behaviour.'

Ruth interrupted, 'I think they felt sorry for him, or at least Janet did.'

Andy was very interested. 'Do you have a photograph of him?'

'No. He stayed inside the Kombi virtually all the time. Our photos of this part of our journey are largely of the sights, with occasional ones of ourselves and Ken and Janet.'

'Would you recognise him if you saw a photo of him?'

'Probably not. He kept very much to himself and it was clear that he did not really want to be seen by anyone. This was particularly true along the main trunk route from Peshawar, across Pakistan, and on towards Delhi. Near Rawalpindi, when we visited the archaeological site of the ancient Indus Valley city Taxila, he remained completely hidden in the VW. Standing near the vehicle, one would not have known anyone was in the car. I recall that he did emerge a little more freely after we had visited the Indian planned city of Chandigarh and we were well on our way up the road into the Himalayan foothills towards Shimla. Back in Pakistan, he seemed particularly cautious.'

'I'm a little curious. Why did you take this detour east into the Himalayas?'

'That's easy to answer—the mystery of Tibet, the possibility of seeing a little of the Himalayas and a remote exotic location. Remember that in 1968, China was closed to the world, and Tibet even more so after the Chinese invasion in the 1950s. The Sutlej River, which the upper Shipki La road follows, has its source in Tibet in the holy Lake Manasarovar, which is not far from Mount Kailash—a sacred place for several religions, including Buddhism and Hinduism. Many overland travellers go on to Nepal. We had arranged to ship our car to Australia from Bombay. A detour to Nepal would have taken us a long way out of our way, and we did not have time. What attracted me initially to the Shipki La detour was the minor road leading there, shown on the old ordinance survey map we had bought in London. After Shimla, the road was shown passing along very deep valleys with snow-capped peaks all around and continuing on into Tibet. It was also not too far off our overall destination route.'

'Go on. It's fascinating, and possibly relevant to my investigation.'

'The road which snaked as it climbed steeply towards Shimla was very busy. We saw at least one accident—a cyclist hit by a car. Fortunately the rider was okay, but the front wheel of his bike was a mess. We knew that Shimla was the summer capital of the British Raj in colonial times, and we enjoyed viewing briefly some of the more important buildings from that time. Again we were off the main tourist route. We only saw one white face there—a Danish woman married to a local Indian.

'After Shimla, the road was much quieter. The surroundings were initially green and forested. We saw a number of relatively tame monkeys beside the road, which shrieked when we drew alongside. At the end of October, the weather was damp and cold, and we were glad to be rugged up in our heated car. In the rain, we came across a man simply clothed in traditional Indian garb, walking along the road with a chained bear. He was soaked to the skin, but did not seem to display any sign of being cold. Presumably, he earned a meagre income by getting the poor animal to perform.

'A little further on, the road, the people, and the surroundings became even more interesting. The road surface was still sealed but very bumpy. It was effectively single-lane but wide enough to accommodate large trucks and had been cut out of the mountainside in British times. There were no safety rails, only intermittent concrete slabs marking the edge of the road. If one met a vehicle, one had to find a slightly wider passing point. On one side of the road, there was a drop of hundreds of metres into the fast-flowing Sutlej River. On the other side, mountain cliffs towered above. We only met a few oncoming vehicles and were relieved when we found suitable places to hover whilst they passed. The edge of the road near the almost vertical drop into the Sutlej, however, was all too close!

'From time to time, the almost sheer drop was replaced by steep hillsides, which were cultivated in narrow terraces. Working there would be back-breaking. We saw relatively few people, but began to notice simple Buddhist shrines and prayer flags on curves in the road. We passed through several small villages that day, and in Kufri, we were excited to read a road sign which read simply TIBET. It didn't specify the distance.

'That night we found a section of road which had been straightened, leaving the old sharp curve on the riverside closed off. We drove in there and camped, lighting a fire for warmth using wood we had collected from beside the road during the day. Whilst we were eating our evening meal in the gathering gloom, a small group of locals walked past and curiously checked us out. We were curious too. They were certainly not ethnically Indian, being more Tibetan in appearance. The woman had a large gold ring through her nose. Even our extra traveller seemed interested in the people. But he still said very little and his face was not very clear in the flickering light of the campfire. Ken and Janet slept in their tent. We slept in our car, and the mystery man slept in the VW. We turned on our car radio briefly and picked up a variety of stations: Pakistani, Indian, and Chinese.

'At Narkanda, we reached a pass with spectacular views on the right of perpetual snow and ice over large sections of the nearby mountains. The road then descended rapidly towards the rushing glacial Sutlej River. All the way along the road from Shimla, people seemed very surprised to see us—particularly in foreign vehicles. What interested us was the change in racial features of the local people as we headed further into the mountains. There were fewer and fewer faces we would have identified as Indian, the majority being of Tibetan appearance. Many of the local women had quite large gold rings through their noses. The only vehicles we saw were military ones and fuel tankers.

'The road followed the river to Rampur, where a huge disappointment awaited us. There was a notice advising travellers that to travel more than a further twenty-two miles on the Tibet road, one needed a permit from the district magistrate. We decided to drive on and investigate.

'When we eventually reached the barrier to the prohibited area, we found a lowered boom gate manned by a friendly Indian lieutenant, who apologised that he could not help us in our desire to reach the border. He told us that he thought the road was surfaced as far as Poo—about twenty miles from the frontier. Whilst we were drinking some tea at the roadblock, a busload of Tibetan-looking passengers arrived, and the lieutenant examined the permits of each person before opening the gate and allowing the bus to continue on its way into the mountains. We decided to visit the magistrate the following day and request the necessary permit.

'We drove back through Rampur and eventually found a small spot just off the road where we camped, attracting the attention of some locals walking past. It was cold, and we went to bed early. We hoped that we would obtain permits, but were not optimistic. If we were unsuccessful, we would simply return to Shimla and drive on to Delhi. The next morning, we discovered that our mysterious travelling companion had disappeared. We never saw him again, and I don't believe Ken and Janet did either.'

Andy interrupted, 'What do you think happened to him?'

'Difficult to say. He may have tried to continue towards Tibet on foot in the hope of hitching a ride. I think it would have been possible to pass by the roadblock by creeping around it at night. If he did this, he would still have had to avoid the military and police every inch of the way, and I doubt there would have been any other possible transport other than an occasional local bus. He might have hitched a ride back to Shimla, but then, why did he not simply wait and travel with us? Our ordinance survey map showed a couple of minor roads in the vicinity, but they were so minor that we did not really notice them as we drove along the main road. I think there were a couple of these near Rampur, and there may have been some further on in the restricted zone.'

'Did you have any discussions with the others about his disappearance?'

'We did. As far as we can recall, they were as mystified as we were. They said that when they took him on board in Peshawar, he was obviously very worried about something and they helped him because they felt sorry for him. Given his accent and age, they guessed he was probably a draft dodger and harmless. They agreed to take him with them as far as New Delhi and no further. I think they had the impression he wanted to get to Nepal. I also think they said that he had appeared less worried after we left the main trunk route from Pakistan to Delhi.'

'Do you think he was involved in drugs in any way, as a user or a peddler or both?'

'We're the wrong people to answer this question! We're very naïve about drugs today, and in 1968, we were even more so. His social behaviour was certainly strange, but physically we did not notice anything unusual. So that possibly answers your "user" question. As far as peddling drugs is concerned, who knows? He carried a cloth hippy-looking bag which he kept with him at all times.'

'Thank you. I suspect that the events you have recounted may be relevant to our investigation, and I'll explain why when you have finished recounting your journey. Did you manage to get permits for the restricted area?'

'Sadly, no—although we guessed this would be the case. After all, the high mountain border area is disputed by both India and China, and it was clear from the military vehicles we saw on the road and the fuel tankers that the whole region near the border would be sensitive militarily. So foreigners, and probably Indians too who did not live in the area, would not be granted access.'

Hugh and Ruth recounted how they had travelled back to Shimla and on to Delhi, where they spent a few days, staying with an Indian American colleague. They had then joined up with Ken and Janet again to complete the journey to Bombay via Jaipur and Agra. From Bombay, they had flown to Sydney via Bangkok. The car was shipped from Bombay. They met no other overlanders on the last Indian section of their journey although they did run into the two boys from Aberystwyth at the shipping terminal in Bombay. They had apparently abandoned their plans to drive to Nepal.

'The only event of major significance en route to Bombay was being attacked by bandits when we were camped about one hundred metres off the main road near Dhulia.'

Andy's ears pricked up. 'Are you sure they were bandits? Could it have been someone believing that you still had the extra passenger with you?'

'No. We don't think so unless that person had engaged a number of local thugs! We were subject to a barrage of stones coming from several slingshots. We were frightened and hurriedly started our cars and drove further on in the dark. The stones made dents in the side of the VW. When we reached Bombay, we recounted the incident to some Indians in the hotel where we were staying, and their immediate response was, "Dhulia—that's bandit country. Indians are advised not to drive through there at night." We were naïve, ignorant, innocent foreigners!'

Although there was still some of the afternoon left, they were all quite tired. Andy, who had taken pages of notes, suggested that if Hugh and Ruth were agreeable, they might meet again the next day when he would provide all the information he had on the missing man and outline the investigations his company had made in 1969. Ruth had an appointment the following day, but agreed to reschedule it so that they could reconvene at 10:00 a.m.

Andy asked whether they might bring with them in the morning photographs of any of the persons they had mentioned in their account of their journey from Teheran onwards. They happily agreed.

# 4

# Afghanistan 1968

THEY MET AS planned the following morning in the same meeting room. Coffee arrived, and Hugh handed over the colour slide photographs that Andy had requested the previous day. Each was in a separate envelope on which was marked the slide number and, where they knew them, the names of the persons photographed. As part of the record of their 1968 adventure, the photographs were very precious to Ruth and Hugh, and Andy promised they would be kept safe. He placed them in a large manila envelope and took them down to reception where he asked that they be couriered immediately to the Sydney laboratory of a specialist photographic company he nominated that also did forensic work. Here they were to be reproduced as enlarged normal photographs. As he left the room, he told Ruth and Hugh that he expected the photographs back by the end of the afternoon.

On his return a few minutes later, Andy began his account of the case.

His client was Esther Blum, a New York widow well into her eighties. She had two sons, Benjamin and Daniel or Dan. The elder son, Benjamin, was drafted and killed in Vietnam. The younger son, Dan, fled to Canada and, from there, to Europe to avoid the draft. His father, now dead, had served with distinction in Korea. When Dan fled, his father felt that the boy had brought shame on the family. At the same time, however, he also experienced the conflicting emotion of relief that their remaining son was not exposed to the risk of death on the battlefield. As a mother, Mrs Blum simply felt relieved that her younger son would not be risking the same fate as his elder brother.

Several times a year, Dan would send a postcard home under fictitious names addressed to himself, and his parents soon realised that they came from their son, who was letting them know that he was okay and giving them some idea as to where he was. Mrs Blum missed him dreadfully, but accepted the situation, and prayed for the end of the war and Dan's return.

'How did he finance himself?' Ruth asked.

'I think I told you earlier that Mrs Blum is wealthy. The family inherited considerable wealth in the early 1960s, and both sons had money of their own. When he fled, Dan took a large sum of money with him as cash in large US dollar notes. This would have lasted him for some time, but eventually it would have run out, even if he was living more frugally than he was accustomed to. A couple of the earlier postcards from London and Amsterdam mentioned working in bars; the later ones either omitted any reference to work or simply mention a "job". The name written on every card was only a first name, and the handwriting varied considerably. The Blums guessed that on each occasion someone else had written the card on behalf of Dan.

'On one occasion, the Blums had a visit from the military, who had obviously been scanning all mail addressed to their home. They went through the names one by one and asked who they were. The parents answered truthfully that they did not know. They were possibly names of college friends. They only had the one visit.

'For about eighteen months, the cards came from Europe, initially from London and then from Amsterdam. Then quite suddenly they came from Turkey, Iran, and Afghanistan. The one from Iran, signed "Amanda", mentioned travelling with friends in an old car. The following one from Kabul referred to having "found a job" and was signed "Will". A later one came from Teheran signed "Chuck", then more from Kabul. All those from Afghanistan bore the same signature—"Will"—and were in the same handwriting. The Blums were convinced that Dan was staying semi-permanently in Afghanistan, but made the occasional journey back to Teheran. Then, in a carefully printed postcard from Kabul, dated 10/5/68, the writer mentioned hoping to travel to India. He also mentioned meeting some Australians who were driving there.'

Andy showed them a photocopy of the card, which read as follows:

*Hi Dan,*

*Greetings from Kabul again. Having a great time here—you should visit! May travel to India and Nepal soon. Will try hitching, otherwise local bus. Some Australians camped here are heading off that way soon too, so I might get a ride with them. Will.*

Hugh and Ruth acknowledged that they were in Kabul around October 5, the date of the postcard, and were prompted to ask how exactly Buffalo Investigations and Forensic Inc. found out that they were in Afghanistan at that time. The answer was simple. A long-standing family friend of Mrs Blum, living in Perth, Western Australia, had come across the book that Hugh and Ruth had written about their two major adventures driving across Eurasia in 1968 and 1999. Knowing Esther Blum's preoccupation with the mystery of her missing son, the friend had told her about the book. With the information in the book, including their address, it was relatively easy for them to track down the authors.

Ruth asked, 'Do you have a photo of Dan?' Andy produced one and showed it to them. The face that greeted them was that of a very young man with short hair, cleanly shaven and tidily dressed.

'Do you think this might be the person who travelled with the other couple after Peshawar? Or do you think it might be one of the others you encountered in Teheran or Kabul?'

It was Hugh who answered. 'You must remember that if we did meet Dan, it was thirty-five years ago. Furthermore, all the young men we met had long hair and sported rather wispy beards. I cannot really say whether or not this is the same person who travelled in the VW with Ken and Janet. Nor can I say whether he is one of those we encountered elsewhere. What you have told us about the missing son is not inconsistent with him being the one who travelled in the VW, but who knows?'

Ruth concurred.

They took a break and ate a light lunch at a small restaurant a couple of blocks away and did not discuss the case until they returned to the hotel meeting room.

When they resumed, Andy began, 'I mentioned the postcards this morning. One thing I did not tell you about was a letter mailed to the Blums late in 1968 from New Delhi. You will see that it is very short and to the point. You will see also that it is undated.' He placed a photocopy in front of Hugh, who read the typewritten letter aloud:

*Dear Mr and Mrs Blum,*

*I need to inform you that someone dear to you is ill and needs urgent medical attention. Whilst the hospital here is convinced that his condition is not life-threatening, he continues to suffer considerable pain over much of his body. The treatment available in New Delhi is somewhat limited, and advice he has had is that he should fly to Europe*

JOHN POLLARD

*for treatment. I am therefore asking you on his behalf to forward $50,000 to the following Swiss bank account with Stefan Dreher Private Banking Schweiz AG:*

*CH73 0054 40A1 0246 0130 2*

*Yours sincerely,*
*Abe Johnston*

'When the Blums received this letter, they pondered what to do. Was it their son seeking financial help? Was it somebody else who knew they were wealthy seeking to extract money from them? There was no way they could tell. The privacy rules of the Swiss banking system would not permit the bank to reveal the name of the account holder. Eventually, parental concern overruled other considerations and they sent the money. There were no further letters from Abe Johnston.

'I should now tell you about the investigations our company made in 1969 and 1970. The Blums approached our company in the middle of 1969 to investigate the whereabouts of their son. They believed that he was still alive, and they would not accept that he might have encountered foul play. Our investigator was Tom Childs, whom I never met, because he died before I joined the firm. Like all investigators employed by Buffalo Investigations and Forensics, he left a detailed record of all the work that he did on the case as well as a few tentative conclusions.

'Tom travelled to Kabul in July 1969. He visited all the likely hotels in the city, interviewing staff and showing them Dan's photo. He visited the police and the various hospitals. None of these enquiries produced anything. Tom also visited the government department which kept records of visas issued by the Afghan embassies around the world. There was no record of a visa being issued to a Dan or Daniel Blum. Assuming that the records were complete, Tom's conclusion was that Dan was travelling on a false passport. The officials were helpful, but steadfastly refused to give Tom access to the visa application photos of all persons granted visas in the two years prior to 1968, arguing that they were not permitted to do so. Of course, even if they had given permission, his appearance might have changed. He could well have grown a beard and possibly long hair.

'Tom continued his investigations in Kabul for three weeks. He visited the official campsite and met two young American men who had been staying there for over a year. They would most probably have met Dan had he been staying at the campsite. He showed them the photo of the clean-shaven young Dan and pumped them for information, but received little cooperation. Whether they were draft dodgers nervous about his questions or whether they knew more than they were letting on was not clear. He suspected the latter, but had no way of forcing them to come clean with him.

'Tom also took photos of the young men, unbeknown to them. He did this over several days, hoping also to obtain images of anyone else they associated with—or even Dan himself. He obtained the photos of a few others, but the encounters in the main seemed to be casual ones between campers. There were however two photos, taken on different days, which included images of a better-dressed man speaking with them. He looked slightly older and had a prominent scar on his face. He certainly did not appear to be attired like a camper. From a distance, Tom gained the impression that on both occasions he was arguing forcefully with the Americans. Tom then carefully did the rounds of the Kabul hotels again, interviewing staff, and discovered where the man was staying. He gave a substantial tip to the man who provided the information and instructed him not to reveal their discussions. The name of the guest as shown in the hotel records was George Williams, and Tom was told that he had stayed there frequently over several years.

'Before leaving Kabul, Tom revisited the visa officials who had previously been helpful and asked for information about George Williams. This time, the officials were more reticent, and it took some persuasion and the exchange of several hundred Afghanis before they agreed to help. It emerged that George Williams held a UK passport and, on several occasions, had obtained multiple-entry visas for Afghanistan.

'Satisfied that he had about as much information as he was likely to obtain during his visit, Tom returned home. He still had more to do before reporting to the Blums. He suspected that the man recorded in two of the camp photographs, George Williams, might have something to do with the case. If he and the young Americans were involved, as Tom was beginning to suspect, George Williams would already know about his—Tom's—enquiries at the campsite. He hoped the hotel employee had not revealed anything. If he had, George Williams would almost surely be aware that for some reason he was being investigated.

'Back in Buffalo, New York, Tom immediately made contact with a friend employed by a major investigation agency in London requesting help. On the phone, the London friend could not help. The name George Williams meant nothing, even when, as they spoke, he scanned his computer. Tom agreed to e-mail the two photos he had, and this brought an immediate response.

'The man Tom knew as George Williams was actually born Patrick O'Connell in Liverpool in 1934. As an adolescent, he had had a number of encounters with the law as a result of his increasingly violent acts. Later, as a young man, he had been sentenced to seven years' imprisonment for manslaughter arising from a failed armed robbery. He had been released on parole after serving six years. The scar on his face was the result of a gang incident in his youth.

'The family of the man killed in the armed robbery was anxious to keep a track of him after his release and had retained the London company for this purpose. To the agency's embarrassment, he completely disappeared from their radar only six months after his release. Tom's London friend was therefore very pleased to learn the new identity and location of the paroled convict. He promised not to do anything that would interfere with Tom's enquiry, and Tom promised to keep him informed about any developments in the case. There was no record of change of name by deed poll for Patrick O'Connell. So he had either acquired a fake passport or obtained a genuine one based on false information. Either way, Tom's investigations continued under the George Williams name.'

At this stage, the telephone rang. Andy answered it, and when he hung up, he announced that the specialist photography company expected to have the photographs delivered to reception by about 4:15 p.m. He was clearly very keen to see the photographs. So too were Hugh and Ruth, but the three of them would have to wait another hour.

Andy produced a photograph from his file. 'Have you ever seen this man?' They examined the image closely, and Hugh shook his head. The man in the photograph had a prominent scar right down the right side of his face, making his already rather frightening face look even more fearsome. Hugh guessed that the image must be that of the George Williams they had just been discussing.

Ruth kept looking at the photograph, and the two men watched her. Eventually she looked up. 'I have a feeling I have seen him. It's the scar—but where?'

Andy was clearly excited. 'Take the photo home with you tonight and see if you can remember the circumstances. I have another copy.' He then continued his account of the 1960s investigation.

'Tom's guess at this stage was that the missing American was probably involved with George Williams, and Dan's "job" was possibly that of a drug mule between Afghanistan and Turkey for the European market, with George Williams the boss in Kabul. Why Dan had fled Afghanistan and apparently headed towards India was not clear. Perhaps he wanted to quit his "job". Perhaps he wanted to go out on his own or work with another drug baron. All these possibilities were simply based on suppositions. He might not even have met George Williams.'

Tea arrived—proper English tea—and they took a break.

It was close to 4:30 p.m. when a hotel reception staff member knocked at the door and delivered the photographs they were expecting. Andy eagerly opened the package and scanned through the numerous images, passing each in turn to Hugh and Ruth to examine.

The pictures were of course familiar to them, and they saw nothing that surprised them. Andy took back the rather fuzzy photograph of the three young Americans at the Kabul campsite and continued to look at it for some time. 'I'll ask for some forensic work on this picture. May I keep the colour slide two more days and send it back to the laboratory? It will be safe.'

Receiving nods from Ruth and Hugh, he scribbled a short note and placed it in a secure envelope and then called reception, asking for the package to be couriered immediately to the laboratory.

'I have relatively little more to report in relation to the company's 1969 investigation. After his initial discussion and e-mail exchange with his London investigator friend, Tom waited a week to see whether that company had any new information on George Williams. The answer was in the negative. So he decided to tell the Blums what he had uncovered, which was remarkably little and had cost them a lot.

'When he met with the anxious parents, he was only too conscious of how little he had to report. He tried to keep only to the facts, which were very few. He showed them the campsite photos he had taken and asked whether they recognised either of the two young men. They did not. He then showed them the pictures of George Williams, and not surprisingly, they did not recognise him either. They were horrified when he told them about the violent background of the man, and their immediate reaction was that their son would not have anything to do with such a person.

'Tom did not mention his suppositions or guesses. Given that he had found out almost nothing definite and at considerable cost to them, he was surprised when the Blums asked him to continue on the case and return to Kabul if he felt that necessary. They still hoped that the mystery would be solved. Tom maintained contact with his London friend over the next nine months, but the contact was of little help in providing an update on George Williams.

'With some misgivings, Tom made another visit to Kabul in the hope of meeting George Williams. He went straight to the hotel where the paroled convict had stayed previously, only to be told that Williams had checked out nearly a year ago and had not been seen since. He checked the other hotels. None had any record of him. The campsite produced nothing, not even the two young Americans. He then visited the government passport and immigration office again and asked to speak with the men he had seen previously. They were no longer there, and the man he spoke with absolutely refused to cooperate.

'The investigation seemed to have come to a dead end. It was with some trepidation and sadness that he reported back to the Blums two weeks later and presented them with yet another substantial bill. He indicated that he could do nothing more. He suggested that they contact him if they received any additional information that might help. It might then be possible to reopen the case. Mr Blum died two years later.

'That was the end of the case until the Western Australian woman contacted Mrs Blum, and Buffalo Investigations and Forensics approached you.'

Ruth had a burning question. 'You told us about the letter requesting or demanding $50,000 but you said nothing more about it in your subsequent account of the initial investigation.'

'Oh, that was an oversight. The Blums were somewhat embarrassed when they showed Tom Childs the letter and told him how easily they had parted with the money. Tom wrote to the bank asking for information, telling the officials that his enquiry related to a missing person investigation and possibly murder, but the bank insisted on maintaining client confidentiality. If the enquiry had come from a government, they might possibly have been more forthcoming. Tom had the letter examined for fingerprints and these are in the case records. There were three sets: those of Mr and Mrs Blum and those of someone else, probably the unknown sender alias Abe Johnston. They were definitely not those of Daniel Blum.'

'Could the military police not have examined the postcards for Dan's fingerprints?'

'Maybe they did, but by then, he had fled to where he could not be arrested. Maybe they didn't, or the postcards had too many other fingerprints on them. Who knows?'

'Thanks.'

'I am hopeful that the photographic lab will have their results back to me by late tomorrow afternoon or Friday morning. There is nothing we can do in the meantime. So I think we should call tomorrow a rest day. Okay? I am assuming that you are willing to continue to help us—a bit presumptuous of me, I'm sorry.'

By now, Ruth and Hugh were beginning to be rather fond of Andy, and they indicated that they were happy to continue with their assistance. They were also becoming intrigued by the case. They felt that they should offer to show Andy something of Sydney and/or its surrounds on their 'free day'. So they were pleased when he accepted their invitation to be shown something of the beauty of the Blue Mountains seventy-five kilometres to the west. He responded by offering a slap-up dinner at the hotel when they returned from the mountains.

# 5

# Fuzzy Photographs

RUTH AND HUGH collected Andy from his hotel at 9:30 a.m., and the three headed out of the city along the western distributor and M4 motorway towards the Blue Mountains. An hour later, they stopped at Glenbrook for coffee, before continuing on to Leura, where they turned off left to give Andy his first glimpse of the dramatic sandstone cliffs, characteristic of the Blue Mountains, which drop hundreds of metres into the Jamison Valley below. It may have been his Highland youth, but whatever it was, Andy was delighted by the rugged scenery the World Heritage listed national park presented, and his enjoyment grew as they continued on around the scenic route to Echo Point near Katoomba. It was a beautiful sunny day, and the renowned Three Sisters with the grandeur of the valley beneath and beyond took his breath away. He snapped numerous photographs.

After a snack lunch near the Three Sisters—the rocky cliffs symbolic of the Blur Mountains—they took the Scenic Railway to the valley floor below. Originally built in the early twentieth century to bring coal to the top of the cliff and converted in the 1930s to carry passengers, the cable-driven 'train' descends very rapidly at almost forty-five degrees through a narrow crevice in the cliff with a head-height overhang. Andy grinned when a large group of Japanese tourists shrieked as the 'train' accelerated into the steepest part of its descent through the low overhung section. At the bottom, they strolled through the rainforest and inspected the disused coal mine shafts before returning to the top in the Swiss-built cable car.

Ruth and Hugh always liked to take visitors to the lookout at the end of the Victoria Falls Road near Mount Victoria, and it was here that they headed after a quick call at Govett's Leap on the north side of Blackheath.

The unpaved road to their favourite lookout does not encourage a large number of tourists, which is remarkable as the view of the Grose Valley is superb and the calls of the bellbirds in the valley below are crystal clear.

It was then time to drive back to Sydney.

At the Wentworth Hotel that evening, Andy was a generous host, who selected an excellent Australian red wine, which he had only discovered soon after his arrival a few days previously. They did not discuss the investigation—that could wait until the morning. Instead, in a friendly relaxed atmosphere, they revealed more of their backgrounds and personal lives. It was good to have a break from the intense discussions of the previous two days.

When they met again the following morning in their usual meeting room, the promised digitally-enhanced photographs had still not arrived. Andy called the company and was told that the photographs had just left by courier. They should be there within half an hour. They ordered coffee and waited.

The package arrived, and it seemed that Andy was almost trembling as he opened it. There were several images. The first was an image of the three Americans, much improved from the rather foggy slide Hugh and Ruth had provided. All three young men were very much clearer and their features could be reasonably well discerned. From his briefcase, Andy pulled out the photographs of the two Americans taken in 1969 and placed them on the table alongside the new picture.

'Are any of the men in the photo we've just received the same as in Tom's pictures?'

Ruth was the first to respond. 'I think the one closest to the camera in our enhanced picture is the same as the one further away in the other closer investigation photo.' The other two agreed.

'What about the second American in the investigation photo?'

'If he is in our photo, my guess would be that he is the one in the middle,' was Hugh's response, but Ruth was not sure. She peered more closely at the photographs and, after a pause, gave her guarded answer: 'Perhaps.'

Andy was inclined to Hugh's view. 'So who is the third man in your photo? Is he relevant to our investigation? Is he our missing man? Are any of them relevant to our case?'

He pulled out another two images from the envelope that had just arrived from the forensic photography company. At first glance, they seemed identical to the photo they had just been examining. But on closer scrutiny, he realised that these two photographs were different. The beards of the three men had been removed, and in one of the pictures, their hair had also been shortened and tidied.

He picked up his briefcase and, fossicking nervously through one of the files, produced the photograph of the missing young man provided so many years ago by his parents. He placed it between the two forensically adjusted images. Whilst the old photograph was sharp and clear, the digitally adjusted photographs were a little fuzzy, particularly where the beards had been removed. The face in Hugh and Ruth's forensically adjusted photo appeared slightly thinner, but the bone structure and overall appearance were very similar.

'I think we may have our man! What do you think?'

It was not possible to determine other characteristics of the man such as height from the photographs. However, the circumstances and the photographic similarities made the answer to his question as 'very likely'.

Andy was clearly happy with the photographic evidence. 'I think we have had a very successful morning's work. You have been most helpful, and I'm sure Mrs Blum will be very appreciative. Thanks so much. Let's go downstairs and have an early lunch!'

Andy urged them not to be shy ordering, and they ended up eating a very filling three-course meal—something they normally never did in the middle of the day. Their host ordered champagne, and the three became very relaxed over a meal that lasted a couple of hours.

Andy was booked to fly back to New York the following evening, and he planned to complete his report in the morning. He thanked Hugh and Ruth again for all that they had done and for giving up three days to the investigation. He gave a short recap of what they had achieved and mentioned two areas where they might still be able to help: further information about the couple they had travelled with after Afghanistan, and where Ruth had seen the scarred man pictured in the earlier investigation photographs if indeed she had ever seen him.

It was with some sadness they said their farewells. Ruth and Hugh both now regarded Andy as a friend, and it seemed that Andy felt the same way about them. As they shook hands warmly, Hugh said, 'We've really enjoyed this week, and I hope we meet up with you again sometime soon.' And Ruth continued, 'I know we will.'

'Aye. I'm sure we will,' was Andy's response.

Early the following Wednesday morning, there was a knock at Hugh and Ruth's door. It was a courier delivering a slim A4-sized package from

Andy. Inside were photographs of George Williams with his scarred face, the authentic photograph of the missing young man provided by his parents decades earlier, the enhanced version of their own colour slide of the three Americans together with the same photograph showing the young men with their beards digitally removed. Most importantly from Ruth and Hugh's point of view, the package enclosed also the original colour slide that they had forgotten to claim on the Friday when they said 'au revoir'. Accompanying these items was a short handwritten note from Andy:

*Dear Ruth and Hugh,*

*Let me first say again how much I have enjoyed meeting you both and getting to know you. Thank you so much for all your help in relation to my work and for your kindness in showing me the Blue Mountains. I really enjoyed that day.*

*Enclosed are some photos that appear to be significant to the case. If they jog your memories in any way—even if what you recall seems insignificant—please e-mail me. Sorry I forgot to give you back your slide on Friday. Here it is!*

*I'll keep you informed of any significant developments.*

*I don't know when we'll meet again. Who knows? If you are travelling in the US and are passing by, please contact me. I'd enjoy showing you around—assuming you'd accept as your tour guide a Scotsman who has only lived in New York State a couple of years!*

*Sincerely,*
*Andy*

# 6

# Eureka!

TWO WEEKS WENT by. Then an e-mail arrived from Andy.

*Hi Hugh and Ruth!*

*I promised to give you an update on the progress with the investigation.*

*I finalised my report as soon as I returned home and promptly delivered it to Mrs Blum. I was surprised how excited she was with what I had gleaned with your help. She examined the digitally enhanced versions of your coloured slide very carefully using a magnifying glass and said she was certain the man we identified in these photos as her son was indeed Dan. I don't think it was just hope on her part.*

*She is most grateful for your help and hinted that she would like to reward you for it (no details!).*

*She seems to think I can work miracles and wants me to continue to work full-time on the case, even though I tried very hard to point out to her that I had little or no information that would allow me to make further progress. Nevertheless, she still pressed me to continue.*

*Mrs Blum is happy for me to keep you fully informed about the ongoing investigation.*

*Andy*

In the days immediately following Andy's departure, Hugh and Ruth had spent a considerable amount of time pondering over the unknowns presented by the investigation and discussing them. Then the practical matters of family and daily living took over. Andy's e-mail suddenly thrust their thoughts back to the case.

Hugh went up to the attic and searched for the two large cardboard boxes that contained miscellaneous papers, travel books, and maps relating to the two major Eurasian motoring adventures they had made in the Mini. He wiped the dust from the lids and started looking through the papers. Each one brought back nostalgic memories of the journeys they had made together. Most of the papers near the top of the first box related to their more recent adventure in 1999 and included the letters he had written (unsuccessfully) seeking sponsorship for that journey. He smiled when he came across the friendly response to one of these, personally signed by a senior financial executive now in gaol for fraud.

He continued studying the papers in each box carefully, so as not to miss anything. Hours passed and eventually he finished the task. He could find nothing that seemed relevant to the case. So he closed the boxes and returned them to the attic. He then pulled out the three bound diary/logbooks that recorded their 1968 journey. Pasted inside alongside the log he had written were postcards, receipts, folded maps, and all sorts of other paraphernalia.

Quite a few of the documents he was now examining had been pasted in the diary/logbook on arrival to Sydney after the completion of the journey, and they were not entirely in chronological order. And like the papers in the box, these miscellaneous pieces brought back memories. So he found the task of working through them slow but not unenjoyable.

Towards the end of the third volume, he came across the menu from a restaurant in Bombay, where they had eaten their last meal before flying on to Australia. That day, they had left their car at the docks ready for shipping. So too had Ken and Janet, whose Kombi would travel to Adelaide. The four of them had dined together before parting ways, and they had all signed the menu and dated it 30 October 1968. And to his surprise, Ken had written their Adelaide address on the back: 'Ken and Janet Hurst, 209 Riley Road, West Croydon (Adelaide)'.

'Eureka! I've found it,' he exclaimed as he rushed from the study to the TV room to tell Ruth.

'Found what?' was her response as she turned momentarily from her television program.

'Ken and Janet's surname and 1968 address.'

'Fantastic. Where was it?'

'On the menu we all signed the last night in Bombay. I'll e-mail the information to Andy now.'

His short e-mail read as follows:

*Hello Andy,*

*I have some good news. I read through every document relating to our 1968 journey and after several hours found the family name and 1968 address of the Adelaide couple on a Bombay menu signed by the four of us the night before we flew out to Sydney (30 October 1968). The details are as follows:*

*Ken and Janet Hurst, 209 Riley Road, West Croydon (which is a suburb of Adelaide).*

*Best regards,*
*Hugh*

# 7

# Searching for Janet

ANDY'S RESPONSE WAS waiting for them when they came down to breakfast the next morning.

*Hi Ruth and Hugh,*

*Thanks for all your work, Hugh. This piece of information could be very helpful indeed. My problem now is to locate Ken and Janet.*

*We don't have an associated company that operates in Adelaide. What I intend to do is contact the forensic photographic group in Sydney and see whether they can provide a suitable contact in Adelaide. If they can, it will probably take the local Adelaide investigator some time to complete his enquiries, particularly given the number of years that have elapsed.*

*I won't contact you until I hear the results of these Adelaide enquiries.*

*Andy*

Three weeks went by before they heard again from him.

*Hi Ruth and Hugh,*

*We're making some progress!*

*The forensic people in Sydney were able to put me in contact with a man who had recently retired from their company and moved to Sellicks Beach just south of Adelaide to be near his daughter and grandchildren. He agreed to undertake the search and has just reported back to me.*

*Using information provided in electoral rolls and old telephone directories, and from meetings with past neighbours and other sources, he discovered that Ken and Janet did in fact live at that address until 1970. After that, they moved several times, and he was able to locate each of these* addresses. Suddenly around 1985, the trail seemed to go cold. No telephone number was listed under K. T. Hurst. He tried a telephone directory search over a much-wider area in South Australia, but this proved unproductive.

Fortunately, 'Hurst' is not a very common name (unlike 'Smith' or 'Jones'!), and when he tried looking in the 1987 directory for 'Hurst' with initial 'J', he discovered three: J. A. Hurst, J. D. Hurst, and D. J. Hurst. It was the third that proved interesting. People who lived in the street at that time confirmed that D. J. Hurst was a woman named Janet whose husband had died in a car accident and had moved to the apartment a year or so after his death. It is clear that 'Janet' was her middle name. Newspapers from 1984 confirmed the death of Ken Hurst in a head-on collision on the main road to Port Augusta on 3 December 1984.

The neighbours proved very helpful. They reported that Mrs Hurst had remarried in 1990, and they did not know her new married name. They recalled that the wedding took place at the nearby St David's Anglican Church. Our man in Adelaide then made an appointment with the rector and asked to see the marriage register held at the church. The minister was a new appointment and was at first reluctant, but then conceded that there was no real reason why he should not allow access to the register. There were relatively few marriages solemnised there in 1990, and he soon found the record signed by 'Janet Hurst'. The bridegroom was 'John Albert Stokes'.

It did not take the Adelaide investigator long to track down the couple's new address.

At this stage, he has not made any attempt to make direct contact with Janet and is waiting for instructions from me.

Whilst all this does not prove conclusively that Mrs Stokes is in fact the Janet we want to contact, it seems very highly likely that she is one and the same.

I need to handle this very carefully if I am to get the cooperation of Mrs Stokes. What I plan to do is the following: I shall write a detailed letter along the lines of the one I sent you, but including information about my discussions in Sydney with you. I shall attach copies of the photographs we have identified as being of the missing man and ask whether she believes it is the same person who travelled with Ken and herself in the Kombi from Peshawar. I have already drafted the letter and will have it couriered to the Adelaide investigator, together with the photographs. I shall e-mail him instructions as to how I would like him to approach Mrs Stokes.

*Are you agreeable to me providing her with your contact details in case she wants to check my bona fides or would simply like to have a chat with you?*

*I'm sure Mrs Blum will now be putting even more pressure on me to continue the investigation!*

*Andy*

Hugh and Ruth e-mailed their agreement.

Three days later, around dinner time, the phone rang. The beeps indicated that it was a long-distance call, and it turned out to be Janet, who explained that a private investigator had made contact with her and delivered a parcel from America containing a long letter from a US investigator and photographs. The letter had provided her with their telephone number.

Ruth told Janet that she was turning the speakerphone on so that she and Hugh could both talk with her. Initially the conversation was mainly about their respective families and what had happened over the thirty-five years since they parted in Bombay. Janet had two daughters, and she and her second husband John had five grandchildren between them. Ruth summarised their family. It was apparent that Janet had overlooked the time difference between Sydney and Adelaide, and Ruth was becoming a little concerned that their dinner might be burned. Eventually, she politely suggested that they call back in about an hour, after they had eaten, and Janet, apologising profusely, gave them her Adelaide number.

When they resumed their conversation, it was clear that Janet was concerned about the fact that she had been approached by private investigators and worried about any risks she might run by becoming involved. Hugh and Ruth conceded that they had initially had the same reservations, but these had been allayed when they met Andy, whom they liked and now regarded as a friend. They filled her in with many of the details they had learned in their meeting with Andy and subsequent e-mails, and she started to sound more relaxed about responding to the letter.

'I found the photos interesting. Whilst I cannot be sure, I think that the man who travelled with us is the one with the beard in the photographs, but I can't be sure. It was a long time ago, and a lot of water has flowed under the bridge since then.'

JOHN POLLARD

They continued reminiscing about the journey from Kabul to Bombay. 'It was in Peshawar that we agreed to take the American with us. He seemed rather frightened by something or someone, but did not offer any real explanation. Our guess was that he was a draft dodger and was frightened of being caught by the US authorities. I felt sorry for him, and Ken somewhat reluctantly agreed to take him with us. We ran into him shortly after we were in that Peshawar shop that sold souvenirs and, as we discovered inside, all sorts of weapons. You were there, Ruth, but I think Hugh had gone back to the motor mechanic to check on progress with your car. Do you remember? We bought some enamelled brass pots. I think you did too. There were several rather shady men in the shop, and I felt relieved when we were outside again. It was shortly after this that you went off to join Hugh at the motor workshop and we encountered the American.

'He tended to hide in the back of our VW all the time, and at night when we stayed at those roadside dak bungalows, he usually disappeared until morning for some reason. He always came back, however, to continue the journey with us. I was a little embarrassed when Ken suggested that he make a contribution towards our petrol costs, but he willingly did so. As far as I recall, money did not seem to be a serious problem for him. You may remember that he always carried a hippy type of bag with him wherever he went. He carried everything he possessed in that, including his money.

'We were surprised when he suddenly disappeared after we camped near Rampur—and quite pleased too! Until then we feared we had him with us for the duration! He gave us no indication that he was leaving, and certainly did not say "goodbye" or "thank you".

'Of course Ken and I were much more relaxed after our passenger disappeared, and the remainder of the journey was much more enjoyable. The only excitement was that night, closer to Bombay, when we were attacked by bandits. Do you remember? I think we were all in quite a lot of danger. Fortunately none of us was harmed and we weren't robbed.

'We kept the Kombi for a year after returning to Adelaide before selling it to buy a more conventional small car. By then, number one was on her way.

'It's been great catching up, even if the circumstances are unusual. After talking with you, I feel more comfortable telling the American investigator all that I know about the mysterious American. I think I'll suggest to the local man that I tell him on the telephone, rather than taking time to write it all out, and then having the investigator come back with questions.

'If you're ever in Adelaide, John and I would love to have you stay. I have your address—the American sent it to me. I'll send you ours.'

Hugh and Ruth talked about their conversation with Janet for a long time that night. The chat with her had revived many happy memories of the journey. They recalled many incidents they had shared: encounters with local Indians in small rural villages, simple wells where they filled up their water containers before treating them chemically, visits to the Taj Mahal and the pink city of Jaipur, snake charmers and elephant rides, and the Ajanta and Ellora caves. And all the time the mystery of the missing American hung over them.

# 8

# Recollection

WITH THE MEMORIES of their 1968 adventure and their telephone conversation with Janet very much in their thoughts, Hugh and Ruth both tossed and turned in bed for some time that night before eventually falling into a deep sleep. Both dreamt—mainly nonsense.

When the radio alarm came on at 7:00 a.m., they lay in bed listening to the music for quite some time, waking slowly. Ruth was the first to speak. 'I now know where I saw that man with the scarred face. It was in that shop in Peshawar—you know, the one Janet mentioned last night.'

'Are you sure?'

'Yes, definitely. You'd gone back to check on progress with repairs to the Mini. I was in the shop with Ken and Janet. They were looking at souvenirs near the entrance and I was looking at items on shelves towards the rear. I glanced up when a man emerged from the rear doorway. To my surprise, he was Caucasian and had a very noticeable scar on his face. He seemed anxious not to be seen by us, because he turned around immediately and disappeared again. I thought it strange at the time and I then forgot the incident. I assumed he was either the proprietor of the shop or a customer involved in a more dubious purchase—possibly a weapon. A Pakistani came out a few minutes later and served us. It was in this shop that I bought those brass dishes with their enamel work, which we still have.'

'If you're sure about this, let's look at the implications. The original Buffalo investigator photographed "Scarface" at the Kabul campsite the summer following Dan's disappearance. Scarface was talking to the two young Americans and apparently arguing with them. When we were in Peshawar the year before, you saw him in the shop. That was the same day Ken and Janet agreed to take the obviously frightened American with them in their Kombi wagon. It's either a bit of a coincidence or else Dan was fleeing from Scarface. Given that Scarface knew the other two Americans—admittedly a year later—and was a frequent visitor to Kabul, he probably also knew Dan. My guess therefore is that Dan was not really fleeing American draft dodger investigators, but was running scared of Scarface. If this is true, then Janet and Ken ran a serious risk accepting the American as a passenger in their Kombi—and we, indirectly, were also at risk. You agree?'

'Yes.'

After breakfast, Hugh sent a brief e-mail to Andy.

*Hello Andy,*

*We spoke with Janet in Adelaide last night, and whilst she was initially rather reluctant to become involved, after our chat she expressed a willingness to talk with you on the phone.*

*The three of us reminisced for quite some time and this must have sparked off something in Ruth's memory, because this morning she remembered clearly where she had seen the scar-faced man, Patrick O'Connell alias George Williams. It was in a shop in Peshawar the same day that Janet and Ken met the American—presumably Dan Blum—and agreed to have him travel to India with them. Ruth recalls "Scarface" disappearing back into the rear of the shop when he saw three Western travellers in the shop—as if he did not want to be observed.*

*To us it all seems too much of a coincidence.*

*We look forward to hearing your view!*

*Hugh and Ruth*

Not surprisingly, Andy's response came very quickly.

*Hi Ruth and Hugh,*

*Thanks so much for your help. Special thanks to Ruth in particular! I agree with you that 'Scarface' (as you call him) and the frightened American (probably Dan) being in Peshawar at the same time seems too much of a coincidence.*

*From what you have told me, I think we need to find out where Scarface is now and what he's up to (assuming he is still alive!). I'll try contacting the London investigation company.*

*When I've spoken with our man in Adelaide, I'll try phoning Janet. In the meantime, I'll update Mrs Blum.*

*Andy*

A week went by before they heard from Andy again. By now they were once again engrossed in the mystery and were excited by the contents of his e-mail.

*Hi Ruth and Hugh,*

*I've spoken with Janet and she has confirmed that the photos we believe to be of Dan are probably of the American who travelled with her and her then husband. Of course she couldn't be certain, but was reasonably sure.*

*I've also tried to track down 'Scarface'. I e-mailed the London investigation company to ask whether they had any current information about Patrick O'Connell alias George Williams. The people there all seem to be new. They told me that they had no record under either name. I'll have to follow up with additional information and hope that they can come up with something.*

*As you are aware, I have kept Mrs Blum informed at every stage. She is very pleased with developments to date. So much so that she is insistent that I travel to Pakistan and India (not Afghanistan, I'm glad to say!) and attempt to follow the leads we now have. She has also suggested that, if you are willing, you might come with me—at her expense, of course.*

*I have pointed out to her time and time again that all these events took place 35 years ago and even younger locals who might have encountered Dan or Scarface when they were, say, 25 would now be 60. Looking for information would be like looking for a needle in a haystack. But she is adamant. She responds by saying that she is anxious to find out, if at all possible, what happened to Dan. She is wealthy and has no one to leave her money to. She is determined to continue the investigation whatever the cost. So what would your reaction be to revisiting Pakistan and India in about three weeks' time?*

*It's over to you!*

*Andy*

Hugh and Ruth were stunned. A free trip to Pakistan and India, presumably in high-class accommodation! Given recent developments in Afghanistan and Pakistan, they were less than enthusiastic about returning to Peshawar and the North-West Frontier. They were excited, however, by the prospect of revisiting Rampur and the Sutlej River valley in India. Indeed, as early as 1968 immediately following the rejection of their application to travel higher up the Sutlej, Hugh had recorded in his log/diary, 'I should really like to return to this area with a four-wheel-drive vehicle and suitable permits. What we have seen is fascinating. Before the trouble with China, and when Tibet was not Chinese, one could have driven to the frontier and possibly well beyond.'

They discussed the proposal for a couple of days before answering Andy's e-mail. Their response made their position clear. They were enthusiastic about the possibility of following their old route from the Pakistan-Indian border to Shimla and into the Himalayas, but with all the violence in the region, they were not prepared to accept the risks of travelling in north-eastern Pakistan.

Andy understood their reluctance to return to Peshawar and proposed a compromise. He would fly to Peshawar and see what if anything he could learn in that city. He would then come to Delhi to meet them. Here they would take a car with a driver and guide. He would make sure that the guide's English was very good, because they would have to rely on him to interrogate people along their route, and it was most important that the guide fully understood what was required of him and could translate back the answers he received clearly and correctly. This appealed to the Australians, and they immediately agreed. They had about a month before meeting Andy in Delhi.

# 9

# India

WITH LESS THAN a month to get to India and then remain there for an indefinite length of time, Ruth and Hugh had much to do. They visited the travel doctor at Chatswood who advised them on health issues for the northern Indian region and gave them the recommended vaccinations. They also visited the Indian consulate in Sydney to apply for visas, specifying 'holiday' as their reason for travelling there. Then there were their personal affairs. Hugh arranged for their son to manage their financial affairs, and their youngest daughter agreed to move back home to manage the house. Their adult children were somewhat mystified by their sudden decision to fly to India for an indefinite period and, with the short notice, were less than convinced by the explanation 'holiday'.

Andy promised to arrange business-class flights from Sydney to Delhi with open-ended return dates and to book hotel accommodation in Delhi for several days prior to his anticipated arrival from Peshawar, where he would be making local enquiries.

With the exciting prospect of making a return visit to Shimla and travelling along the Sutlej River again, Hugh set about learning as much as he could about the river, its source, the valley and its people, and the towns. When they had travelled there in October 1968, he had not made any serious prior study of the region. The decision to drive there had been very much a spontaneous pragmatic one. They did not have enough time to drive all the way to Nepal, and he had been concerned how well their little car would withstand the additional distance and altitudes. The drive to Shimla and beyond was both closer and shorter.

He looked again at the maps they had used. The 1944 ordinance survey map of the region south-east of Shimla showed the source of the

Sutlej as Rakas Lake (Langak Tso in Tibetan), which is fed by waters from the very holy pilgrimage Lake Manasarowar (Tso Mapham in Tibetan). He discovered that along its course to join the Indus, the river enjoys a variety of names, including Langchen Khambab in Tibet. With its scale of 1:1,000,000, the corresponding 1961 map of the Sutlej from where it breaks through the Himalayas at the Shipki pass into India did not provide much more detail either. The main road from Shimla to the Shipki La pass was shown largely as a small red dotted line, as were a couple of apparently insignificant side roads that seemed simply to disappear; they presumably led to small mountain villages on tributaries of the Sutlej.

References he found elsewhere to the source of the Sutlej were often vague: 'Its source is near Lake Rakshastal in Tibet, China, near [the very holy pilgrimage mountain] Mount Kailas.' Others were more definite: 'Lake Manasarovar lies at 4,556 metres above mean sea level, making it the highest freshwater lake in the world . . . It is connected to nearby Lake Rashastal by the natural Ganga Chhu channel. Manasarovar is the source of the Sutlej River.'

The book he found particularly interesting in his research was by Alexander Gerard, entitled *Account of Koonawur in the Himalaya*, published in 1841, which records the surveyor's journeys in the Sutlej region in 1817 and 1818. The names shown on his detailed map for the river begin high in Tibet as Langzhing Kampa, then successively Muksung, Sampoo, Zung Tee, and Sumuaruna, and finally Sutroodra or Sutlug. Over much of its mountain length, Gerard estimates the fall of the Sutlej, usually a raging torrent, as about fifty-five feet in every mile or about ten metres per kilometre. He reports a couple of hot springs adjacent to the river.

There are several interesting remarks about Lake Manasarovar. In a footnote, he states, 'Mansurowur has always been reckoned by the Hindoos to be the source of the Sutluj, although European geographers were of a different opinion. Captain Webb thinks that there is a considerable difference of level between the two lakes, and that the superfluous water of Mansurowur is drained off by a subterraneous passage, and I fancy he is right.' In the body of the text, Gerard records that 'Mr Moorhead could discover no outlet of this lake, although he heard that a communication formerly existed between Mapang [Mansurowur] and Lanka [Rakshastal]; my information is positive, that about twenty years ago, a stream, which was rapid, and crossed by bridges, ran from it into Rawun Rudd [Rakshastal], but that it has since dried up, and the Lamas who reside on the banks have an idea that a subterranean communication exists.'

Shipki also merits a number of references. 'Shipke is a large village in the small district of Rongzhoong . . . The houses here, which are very much scattered, are built of stone and flat-roofed . . . It is a populous place; we counted upwards of eighty men who, on our arrival, came to meet us, being the first Europeans they had ever seen. The Tartars pleased us much, having none of that ferocity of character so commonly ascribed to them.'

The reason travellers in the 1960s beyond Rampur were required to have permits was the war between India and China in 1962 over this mountainous region with its disputed border. Chinese troops marched in, and the situation was probably aggravated by the acceptance by India a couple of years earlier of the Dalai Lama, following the Chinese move into Tibet in 1956.

Conflict in the region appears to go back much further. According to Gerard, 'the Tartars are very different in appearance from the inhabitants of lower Koonawur [lower Sutlej valley]; and all those of Busehur [higher up the valley] were formerly under the Chinese. There are seven villages of them on the left bank of the Sutluj, which used to be a scene of contention between these two states; the Busehurees were the aggressors, and the Chinese retaliated by bringing an army at three different times as far as Murung, and plundering some of the adjoining places. Both parties, about ninety or a hundred years ago, found it to their mutual advantage to conclude a commercial treaty, since which time there has been peace and a great deal of intercourse between them. The above seven villages were afterwards given up by the Grand Lama of Lahassa [Lhasa], for the support of the Tuzheegung Temple.' Gerard noted a number of Lama temples along the Sutlej.

He also reported on a number of cultural features of the 'Tartar' people. 'Their religion is Lama, and they are very superstitious, paying great regard to lucky and unlucky days . . . In the upper parts of Koonawur it is common for one person from each house to be educated to the church, which is likewise the case in Thibet.' At mountain passes, shughars were constructed where believers placed pieces of quartz or coloured rags on poles to ensure safe passage. Gerard also noted the prayer wheels in the Lama temples and smaller ones carried by travellers. He also observed at Soongnum three prayer cylinders driven by water using the watermill principle and at Nisung several driven by wind.

'It is the obligatory duty on all Lamas to perform the circuit of Mapang [Mansurowur] and Kangree [Mount Kailas], and the oftener this is done the better, and some people make a point of going round both every year. The most religious make the circuit of Mapang seven times, which is considered a sacred number.

'The number of inhabitants to a house was only ascertained in a few places, but the mean of these in various parts of Koonawur gives six, which will not appear too many, since polyandry, or plurality of husbands, prevails.' Polyandry was also well-known in Tibet.

Access by Europeans to Tibet was strictly controlled. 'The Chinese Tartars, on this remote frontier of their vast empire, are just as vigilant respecting the non-admission of strangers as their countrymen at Pekin: no sum of money, however great, will bribe them to infringe the orders of their superiors. Last years I reached the limits of their country in four different quarters, but was not allowed to advance a step further; the same occurred in 1818, when my brother and I visited Shipke and were the first Europeans they had ever seen . . . And lately, two pilgrims on their way to make the circuit of Mansurowur were stopped at Shipke, being taken for Europeans in disguise.'

Rampur, where Hugh and Ruth tried to obtain travel permits in 1968, gains a number of mentions. In Gerard's opinion, 'Rampoor is a poor-looking place, consisting of about one hundred houses, and situated upon the left bank of the Sutroodra or Sutlug. It contains seven or eight shops, but few articles of any kind are to be got . . . The houses are generally large, well built of stone, and slated like those of most villages in this part of the country . . . Under the Rajah's palace, which is at the northern angle of the town, there is a Jhoola or rope-bridge across the Sutlug which leads to Kooloo.' Hugh's log/diary entry in October 1968 records his impressions of the town: '[Rampur] was much larger than immediately apparent from the road. All the shops etc. were off the main road down footpaths. There were several Buddhist temples.'

The roads Captain Gerard travelled were generally narrow footpaths skirting precipices. They were never very good for long because of the many large rockfalls that occurred all the time. Reading this, Hugh recalled the numerous boulders and smaller rocks they encountered when they drove the narrow tarmac road to Rampur. The 'roads' that Gerard walked had cairns of stone within sight of one another so that travellers could discern the route even after a major rockfall had destroyed the track. He describes a variety of primitive bridges in the Sutlej valley, including two made of twigs and vines in the vicinity of Shipki.

None of this seemed likely to assist them or Andy in the investigation, but helped them understand more fully the valley that had fascinated them thirty-five years earlier and continued to hold a mysterious attraction for them.

The four weeks passed quickly, and soon Ruth and Hugh were on their Singapore Airlines flight to Delhi via Singapore. When they touched down in the Indian capital, they took a taxi to their hotel. As their cab struggled through the city traffic that was far heavier than they remembered from 1968, the exotic aroma of the Indian subcontinent immediately reminded them of their previous visit and their belief that it was part of the magnet, which, over centuries, kept so many Europeans captive to the subcontinent.

Mrs Blum was certainly generous in allowing them to stay in the five-star Le Méridien Hotel in Ashoka Road in the centre of the city. In 1968, Hugh and Ruth had stayed with the family of an American academic colleague, and over two days, his driver had shown them the more important tourist sights of the city. They felt that revisiting these sites was an appropriate way of filling in the couple of days they had before Andy arrived. So through the hotel, they arranged a car with an English-speaking driver. They did not really need to list where they wanted to go, as he already knew all the main tourist sights.

What they had forgotten in the intervening years was the grandeur of the official buildings, constructed in the last years of British rule on a huge scale in a European style but with Indian touches. It was clear that the British expected to stay indefinitely. All these sites were in the New Delhi area and easily reached from their hotel. They recognised each from their colour slides of 1968, which they had looked at only recently: the magnificent India Gate, Connaught Place, Parliament House, the president's residence, and the Governor's House.

After a hot Indian curry lunch at the hotel, washed down with ice-cold beer, they resumed their tour, visiting some of the sites in the old city north of New Delhi—further away but still readily accessible—the red fort, built like many other buildings on the Indian subcontinent in red sandstone by the Mughals in the seventeenth and eighteenth centuries; the nearby Ashoka Pillar, one of a number of such pillars in India, dating back 1,600 years or more; the Jama Masjid (mosque), largest in India, and not unlike the huge mosque they remembered in Lahore.

They caught sight of the Yamuna River a couple of times—one of the three holiest rivers in India. An important tributary of the Ganges but badly polluted even before it reaches Delhi, the Yamuna originates at the base of a glacier high in the Himalayas not far from the Sutlej. Another of the Ganges' numerous tributaries, the Ghaghara has its source on the Tibetan plateau near Lake Mansarovar and enters India by way of Nepal.

Ruth and Hugh were then driven back towards New Delhi to visit the 1724 Jantar Mantar astronomical observatory before heading south-east to view the Humayun tomb, built in the red sandstone of the Mughal period.

By this time, they were ready to return to their hotel to shower and relax before dinner. There was a message waiting for them from Andy: he was on schedule to arrive as planned two days later in the evening. There were no direct flights. To get to New Delhi, he had to take an eleven-hour Emirates flight via Dubai, a long journey to travel a relatively short distance! He said nothing about his time in Pakistan.

With two more days before their friend's arrival, they booked the same driver to take them to Agra the next day, planning to relax by the hotel pool the day of Andy's arrival and possibly do a little shopping. With a drive of more than three hundred kilometres each way to visit the Taj Mahal, it would be a long day, and their driver suggested departing at 7 a.m.

They were punctual and so was he.

In 1968, they had driven to Agra by way of the 'pink city' of Jaipur and nearby Fatehpur Sikri with the best Mughal ruins in India—a magnificent city in pink sandstone, built to celebrate military victories, but abandoned only thirty years later because of lack of water. Apart from the colour slide photographs of the numerous beautiful buildings in Jaipur, they also had a simple black-and-white snapshot of the two of them with Ken and Janet enjoying an elephant ride near the palace in Jaipur and another of a snake charmer. Between Jaipur and Agra, they had camped beside the road in a reserve where tigers were reputed to roam, but fortunately, they encountered none.

This time they were taking the direct road from Delhi to Agra. The traffic on the Indian roads was far heavier than they remembered. There were many more cars and the trucks still bore their essential 'HORN PLEASE' sign. In Agra, they ate an early lunch—a hot curry that they enjoyed—before heading to the Taj Mahal. The city seemed busier, dirtier, and more industrialised than in 1968, and this appeared to have affected the famous mausoleum as well. Nevertheless they still took the compulsory tourist photographs.

After more than six hundred kilometres on busy roads and wandering around the Taj Mahal in the heat for an hour and a half, Hugh and Ruth were exhausted when they eventually got back to their hotel late that evening. They showered and ordered a room-service Western meal before collapsing into bed.

They slept in the next day and did not leave the hotel, relaxing instead by the hotel pool. Andy telephoned their room around 8:30 p.m., and they arranged to meet downstairs for a drink and chat. His visit to Pakistan had not produced any useful information. It was, as he had predicted in his meeting with Mrs Bloom, 'like looking for a needle in a haystack' and possibly worse. He had done the rounds of all the likely looking tourist shops in Peshawar and had drawn a blank. No one in the 50-plus age range recognised either Dan or Scarface—or at least no one admitted to it. A couple were quite aggressive, possibly believing him to be an American, and he had to back off.

He also did the rounds of likely hotels. An elderly cleaner he approached in one of the better establishments seemed to show a flicker of recognition when shown a Scarface photograph, but then denied ever having seen the man. The younger hotel manager was polite and tried to be helpful, but not surprisingly, the guest register no longer existed for 1968. The manager suggested speaking with the police who collected hotel guest lists. Andy tried this, but they claimed to have more important matters to attend to and refused to help.

He had hired a car to take him to Lahore, from where he would fly out to meet Ruth and Hugh. His rather fierce-looking driver was less than friendly initially, but softened somewhat when he learned that Andy was Scottish rather than American or English. Given the size of Lahore, the chance of turning up anything of use seemed remote. But to keep faith with his client, he did try, not very enthusiastically, and found nothing. Now they were back together in New Delhi.

Andy had brought a reasonably detailed road map of northern India with him, and they discussed how they would approach the Indian part of the investigation. He already had a guide, driver, and large car organised and was assured that the guide spoke and understood English very well. Andy had also clearly done a lot of research on the major cities south along the main highway from Pakistan.

'If our suspicions are true, Scarface would have to have taken the main Trunk road south from the Pakistan border. I believe that the important cities where he may have stayed overnight—Amritsar,

Jalandhar, and Ludhiana—are so large that it would be pointless trying to search from hotel to hotel. My guess is that before Shimla, we are unlikely to find out anything of value. Shimla is about 220 miles from here, and we could get there comfortably tomorrow. I suggest, however, that we don't go as far as that, but stay overnight in Chandigarh. The reason I suggest this is that I would like to train and test our guide in making enquiries. We could get him to do this in Chandigarh and observe how he performs. Chandigarh would have been rather smaller when you travelled there in 1968, but even today with a population of slightly more than half a million, it is much smaller than Amritsar, Jalandhar, and Ludhiana. Our guide of course has already been informed as to what he will be required to do.'

'Back in the States before I flew to Pakistan, I managed to obtain a list of the better hotels in Chandigarh which were there in 1970. We will start with these. You never know what may emerge—but I think our real hope of progress will be when we get near Shimla and beyond. I trust you are happy with these plans. We'll need at least two full days in Chandigarh.'

'What you say makes sense,' was Hugh's response. 'My only concern is that our guide may get accustomed to drawing blanks and, as a result, may miss something further down the track.'

'I hope not. I intend to be with him every time he approaches and questions someone, and I'll be watching the person's reactions closely. If I see any indication that follow-up questions are needed, I'll be giving him the questions to put to that person immediately.'

# 10

# Shimla Revisited

ANDY HAD ARRANGED to meet their guide and driver immediately after breakfast at eight thirty. He told Ruth and Hugh that he wanted to spend half an hour with the man discussing what was required of him and checking whether he would be up to the job. So they had plenty of time to pack.

Three quarters of an hour later, Andy telephoned from the lobby and suggested that they meet at the car in fifteen minutes. He was happy with the guide's English and English comprehension. He told them that the guide Maruti seemed pleased about the additional responsibilities he would have and the importance of his work, and this boded well.

They began the journey to Chandigarh. Anupam was a careful driver, unlike many others on the main road north. The traffic was heavy and slow moving. Fortunately, the air conditioner worked well, and the thick fumes from the surrounding vehicles were barely detectable in the cabin as they crawled out of the city.

Andy and Maruti continued discussing the role Maruti would play in the investigation, and it was obvious to Hugh and Ruth that the guide was indeed feeling very important and keen to undertake his responsibilities. Andy emphasised once again that he would have to show the photographs to many people, and very likely none would recognise the men. Maruti was not to become discouraged.

Whilst driving, they discussed whether it was even worthwhile making enquiries in Ambala since it was a city of over a million people. If Scarface had travelled to Shimla and up the Sutlej River, as they suspected, he probably would not have travelled as far south as Ambala, but he may have done so subsequently. So might Dan have done if he was later travelling with Scarface. Instead of making visits to hotels and police, Andy decided, therefore, to place an advertisement in the main local newspaper with photographs of the two, giving a few details and asking anyone recognising either of the men to telephone him. He offered a small reward for information, recognising that this might produce a number of hoax calls and false leads. Maruti proved very helpful locating the newspaper office and placing the advertisement. After a light lunch, they continued on to Chandigarh.

Hugh and Ruth had chosen to visit Chandigarh in 1968 because it was publicised as the first planned city in India post independence in 1947, designed by the Frenchman Corbusier. It was also more or less on their route to Shimla. They remembered it being small, tidy, and clean. Thirty-five years later, it enjoyed the reputation of being the cleanest city in India with one of the highest per-capita incomes.

Entering the outskirts of the city thirty-five years later, Hugh and Ruth remarked how much Chandigarh had grown since their earlier visit. On that occasion, they had stayed in a cheap hotel. They could not recall where they stayed, or whether the passenger in Ken and Janet's Kombi had disappeared overnight as he was wont to do. This time they checked into a comfortable recently refurbished hotel for three nights.

Over the next two days, Andy did the rounds of all the hotels on his list, accompanied by Maruti. Each time, he asked to speak with the manager, gave him the name Scarface had adopted, and asked whether he had stayed at the hotel. Not surprisingly, none of the hotels had records of those years. Andy then asked whether there was anyone on staff who would have been employed in late 1968 with whom he might speak. In a couple of cases, the manager was able to find at least one man. With Maruti showing the photographs and Andy directing the questions, they carried out the interviews. Hugh and Ruth did not accompany them on these hotel visits. There was nothing really that they could contribute, and the men being interviewed might feel intimidated answering questions in front of four people, three of them foreigners. Instead they took a guided tour of the centre of the planned city. They recalled it vaguely from 1968. The rest of the time they relaxed in the hotel.

After the first couple of hotels, Andy and Maruti had become well practised in their interviewing. All the hotel managers were cooperative, even interested. The second afternoon, they managed to interview five men. One seemed to show a flicker of recognition when he saw the missing American's photograph, but then decided that he was mistaken. It must have been someone like him. Whether or not he correctly recognised the face in the photograph, the man's vagueness left them convinced that he would not be able to provide any useful information. He showed no sign of recognition when shown the photograph of Scarface. All the other men were cooperative but unable to help.

After two days of enquiries, it was disappointing not to have any leads on the two men of interest. Andy invited their guide and driver to join them in the evening for dinner. The two Indians were clearly reticent to do so, but eventually accepted. It was clear that Andy was very pleased with Maruti's work and he complimented him several times. After a while Maruti, who had become quite relaxed with them in the car, became a little more relaxed at the meal table, and the four of them discussed the work to date and what they should do next. The fifth person at the table, their driver Anupam, still looked uncomfortable. They came to the view that they ought to try visiting the police in the morning and see whether they would be of any help. If nothing of interest emerged from that visit, Andy would place an advertisement in the *Chandigarh Tribune* and at least one other local newspaper, and they would continue on towards Shimla.

The next morning, they were quite surprised when they found that the police showed a lot of interest. The officers were all too young to have been in the force in 1968, however, and they were not able to produce any hotel records other than for the most recent couple of years. Just as they were about to depart and were expressing their thanks to the police, Andy's telephone rang. He answered it and heard an Indian voice, which he had difficulty understanding. He passed the telephone to Maruti, who spoke for a few minutes with the caller, apparently arguing a little. He then covered the telephone and explained the conversation to Andy and the others. 'The caller claims to have some information for us, but is demanding the reward first. It is my opinion that he knows nothing and just wants to get the money. What should I do?'

'Ask him for his name and telephone number and we can call back.'

Maruti did as he was instructed and the line went dead.

'Well, that's the first one. We'll probably have a few more!' was Andy's comment. 'But we had to try.'

With Maruti's invaluable assistance, they placed advertisements in three newspapers and then set out in the direction of Shimla. There were several smaller towns along the National Highway 22 towards Shimla. Kalka, the entry station for the renowned Kalka-Shimla railway, built with great difficulty in British times to facilitate the summer migration from the heat of the plains to the cool of the Himalayan hills of the senior British officials who governed a fifth of the human race, seemed the most promising of these to make further enquiries. It was only a short drive from Chandigarh, and they were there within an hour.

Andy and Maruti were now well practised in their hotel routine, and they started to do the rounds of the small number of hotels in the centre of town. At the third location, they struck pay dirt. An elderly attendant identified Scarface as having stayed at a hotel where he previously worked as a security officer in the hotel's car park. He remembered the man well because of his scar and the threatening, arrogant manner he displayed when the security attendant asked him to move his car a few feet to one side so that there would be space for another vehicle. Scarface refused and later told the hotel manager that the attendant had been rude and insolent. As a result, he had lost his job. The attendant did not know where the unpleasant foreigner was travelling or where he had come from. He could not remember the year. All he could say was that it was a long time ago when he was a much younger man. At least the investigating team now knew their man had been in the area, presumably around the time of interest.

This was an encouraging discovery—their first lead since arriving in India. They ate lunch in a restaurant down the road and then resumed the drive up the winding hill road to Shimla. The steady climb was much the same as Hugh and Ruth remembered it from 1968, but the traffic was much heavier and the drivers crazier. They were glad they had a careful driver. Shimla itself seemed much larger and busier than they recalled.

That evening over dinner, they planned their course of action for the next few days. After their success in Kalka, Andy was keen to do the rounds of the most likely hotels in Shimla that were on his list. He suggested that he and Maruti could do this whilst Ruth and Hugh saw some of the sights of the hill station city. They had spent very little time in Shimla in 1968, and there were many things dating back to the British Raj times that they had not seen and should see on their return. Maruti would be busy with the hotel enquiries, so they would not have the car to drive them around. But this did not matter. Most of the tourist sights were within reasonable walking distance of their hotel, and those slightly further afield were easily reached by taxi.

# 11

# Rampur

MARUTI AND ANUPAM were clearly more comfortable eating their meals at restaurants frequented by other drivers and guides rather than with their clients. The food at these places, presumably, was also more to their liking. So Andy did not prevail on them to join him and the two Australians at meals. The Indians also chose their own accommodation each night. The driver and guide each had a per diem allowance from the car hiring company in Delhi, and if they lived frugally, they would have more money in their pockets at the end of the expedition.

Ruth and Hugh wished Andy good luck at breakfast the next morning, and after a mid-morning coffee, the couple set out to explore Shimla on foot. They spent some time strolling up and down The Ridge and Mall Road, window-shopping and observing the locals.

They also checked out a couple of possible eating places for lunch and decided on the restaurant in what in British times was the Shimla bandstand. Circular in shape and now glassed in, the bandstand held a prominent position near the centre of The Ridge. They were not disappointed in their choice. They were shown to their table beside the window by a friendly waiter. As with virtually all the menus in India, the dishes were largely vegetarian with the occasional chicken offering. This time the menu also included a freshwater fish from one of the nearby rivers, possibly the Sutlej. They only wanted a small meal, so they selected a chicken and corn soup washed down with some Kingfisher beer. Whilst waiting for their food and during the meal, they watched the hundreds of people promenading up and down The Ridge.

After lunch, they took a taxi to visit the viceregal lodge, which they had only seen from the outside in 1968. Located in beautiful grounds a kilometre or so from the centre of Shimla and commanding splendid views, the very grand building has the appearance of a Scottish stately home. Andy would have liked it. First occupied in 1888, it featured electric lights, a novelty at that time. Now the home of The Institute of Advanced Studies, the public are permitted to visit certain rooms on the ground floor. It was only when they wandered slowly through these rooms that Hugh and Ruth realised the importance of this building in twentieth-century Indian and British history, with major figures in the struggle for independence and partition, who met here, featured in the photographs on the walls. It was a very interesting tour.

At dinner that night, Ruth and Hugh told Andy about their tourist activities and the latter filled them in with his day. Unfortunately, he had made no progress in tracking down Dan or Scarface.

'Did you have any responses to the newspaper advertisements?' asked Ruth.

'I turned my phone off overnight. When I switched it on again before breakfast, there was a message telling me that there were three missed calls. There was no further information—the caller or callers had left no messages. My guess is that they came from people with no information hoping to claim a reward. But who knows? I had the phone on all day whilst Maruti was with me, but no one called in response to the advertisements.'

'What are your plans now?' asked Hugh.

'I would like to spend one more day in Shimla and finish off the hotels on my list. Unless something surprising and helpful turns up, I think we should drive on to Rampur the next day. Before moving on, however, I'll place advertisements in several local newspapers. Maybe we'll have greater luck here in Shimla.'

At breakfast the following morning, Andy announced that when he had turned his telephone on before coming down to breakfast, he found that there was a recorded message. It had been recorded only a few minutes earlier. Rather than returning the call himself, he would ask Maruti to do so when they met up with him at 9:00 a.m. Hugh and Ruth were as curious as Andy about this possibly promising call and asked to be present when Maruti arrived. The Scot's response was immediate. 'Of course. You're both part of the team.'

It was with some anticipation that the three of them met Maruti at the car shortly afterwards. The guide dialled the number a couple of times before he received a response, and a reasonably lengthy conversation ensued. He then covered the telephone with his hand and reported his discussion.

'The man is asking about the reward. He lives in Chandigarh and claims that he sold his father's Indian Morris car to the man with the scar.'

Andy was obviously excited. 'Please tell the man that this information is helpful and that I would like to meet with him to get as many details as possible. Please ask him to stay by the phone and we'll ring back in a few minutes—I want to discuss something with Hugh and Ruth and then call him back.'

Andy turned to the others. 'I think this may prove to be important, and I'm thinking of going back to Chandigarh with Maruti and Anupan, possibly today if we can arrange it. Of course you can come along as well, but it's quite a long drive there and back in one day and you'd probably have more fun here in Shimla—but whatever you'd like to do, I'm happy with. I'll also try to meet the parking security man in Kalka again on the way back to Shimla in case any details we obtain from our Chandigarh caller jog his memory.'

'You're sure you won't need us?' asked Hugh. 'Call him back now anyway, and we'll chat about whether to join you or stay here.'

Maruti called the man back on Andy's behalf and arranged to meet him in the early afternoon.

Whilst he was telephoning, Ruth and Hugh made a snap decision. They would remain in Shimla and continue their sightseeing. They had already planned where they intended to go, and there didn't seem to be much they could do to help back in Chandigarh. They farewelled the others and wished them luck.

One of the things they hoped to do was to travel part of the way back towards Kalka on the famous 'toy train', considered the jewel in the crown of the Indian railway system when it was completed one hundred years earlier. The hotel called a taxi for them, and the driver was pleased to help them and act as their guide. When they arrived at the Shimla railway station, the driver led them to the ticket office, but they soon discovered that their hope of travelling on the tiny train would not eventuate. The train was fully booked for the rest of the week and most of the following week. So they consoled themselves admiring the tiny tracks and turntable, watching the train connect to the carriages and observing the lucky passengers climbing on board.

When the train departed, the taxi driver suggested taking them to the monkey temple on Jakhoo Hill overlooking Shimla. It was a steep climb up the hill, and their driver offered to wait for them and take them down again when they were ready. They were only too happy to do this. He warned them to be careful with their glasses—the monkeys like to snatch them. He also warned that it was dangerous to look a monkey directly in the eye, as the monkey interprets this as aggression and responds accordingly. He was serious and they took note.

The final approach to the temple was up a long covered stairway, with monkeys everywhere. About halfway up, Hugh suddenly felt a sudden powerful thump on his back, slumped forward, and uttered a gasp. A large monkey had jumped from the ceiling truss above on to his back and then run off squealing. Hugh recovered quickly and, thinking about the risk of rabies, was relieved to discover that the skin on his back had not been pierced. He watched warily the rest of the way to the top and again on their way down after they had taken their tourist snaps of the temple.

It was lunchtime by the time they got back to central Shimla. They thanked and paid the taxi driver, who was keen to drive them again in the afternoon, but they declined because they planned to visit a couple of the tourist sights in the centre.

Perhaps they were a little unadventurous, but they decided to return to the band pavilion restaurant for lunch. The waiter recognised them immediately, led them to 'their' table, and even recited their meal order from the previous day. They took their time over lunch, again watching people promenade along The Ridge.

First stop in the afternoon was Christchurch, a hundred metres up the road. A neo-gothic Anglican church from the mid-nineteenth century, it brought home to its visitors once again the very British history of this hill station. The rest of the afternoon was spent strolling up and down The Ridge, talking occasionally to some of the local people. On their return to the hotel, there was a telephone message from Andy: 'Don't wait up for us tonight. We'll be quite late. See you at breakfast.'

'Well, he could have told us something about his enquiries in Chandigarh!' exclaimed Ruth. 'Now we'll have to wait till the morning!'

They were down to breakfast early, eager to hear the news from Chandigarh, and it seemed an interminable wait until Andy arrived. As soon as he arrived, Ruth could not contain herself. 'How did your visit to Chandigarh go?'

'Quite well, I think. The journey was certainly worthwhile. The man was clearly genuine—and happy to receive his reward! The car was his father's and he sold it to our Scarface. It seems that it was an early 1960s green Indian Morris Major. The purchaser seemed very keen to buy it in a hurry and paid a little more than our caller expected. Before he paid, Scarface took the car for a test run with our caller in the passenger seat. We showed him the photographs of Dan, but as we might have guessed, he did not recognise him. That's about all we learned from our visit, but it's a good start.'

'Did you manage to talk with the Kalka parking security man?' asked Hugh.

'Yes, but it took some time to locate him again. That's why we arrived back in Shimla so late. We didn't learn anything more from him really. When we asked what type of car it was, he couldn't recall. When we asked whether it was an Indian Morris, he said it may have been. He didn't recall the colour. But at least the information from Chandigarh was helpful.'

'So what next?'

'We complete the rounds of the Shimla hotels today and set out for Rampur tomorrow morning. Okay?'

'That's fine by us.'

Hugh and Ruth had only one more important place to visit in Shimla, its Gaiety Theatre, dating from British times. It was their first point of call that morning. Photographs and programme billboards of the period revealed that young army officers and their wives and even some of the more senior of the British ruling class participated as actors in many of the performances. Rudyard Kipling, as a young man, also acted in the theatre. The Australian tourists were surprised how small and intimate it was.

On the way back to the hotel for lunch, they bought postcards, which they later wrote in their room. As far as family and friends knew, they were simply having a holiday in a region of India they had visited thirty-five years earlier. The hotel reception agreed to mail the cards for them.

At dinner, Andy had little to report. His visits to four hotels had produced nothing. With Maruti's assistance, he did, however, manage to place advertisements in three newspapers widely read in the Shimla region—*Amar Ujala* and *Divya Himalchal* in Hindi, and the *Tribune* in English. After his success in Chandigarh, he did not feel discouraged. The information he had received there and Kalka confirmed that Scarface had definitely been in the area, presumably about the same time Hugh and Ruth had been there. The real test for the investigation team would come when they reached Rampur.

It is said that returning to a place that has happy memories can often be disappointing. When the investigation team set out the next morning towards Rampur, it was immediately apparent to Ruth and Hugh that the area was now far more congested and busy than it was thirty-five years earlier when they only encountered the occasional vehicle. Even as soon as Kufri, they noticed the changes, as the road they followed bypassed the centre of town and they did not have the opportunity to look for the road sign they had photographed in 1968 pointing to Tibet. There were many trucks laden with apples, and they asked Maruti about these. The guide explained that the area is the main apple-growing region for all of India and dates back originally to an American Quaker missionary, Samuel Stokes, who settled there in the early twentieth century. Apparently he later married an Indian woman and converted to Hinduism.

At Narkanda, they could see the distant snow-capped peaks of the Himalaya but were unable to identify the location where they took their 1968 mountain photographs. Highway 22 then descended towards the Sutlej River, and it was not long before they reached Rampur, which like Shimla seemed far larger than they remembered. It was heaving with people, animals, and trucks. They ate a quick lunch at a restaurant on the edge of town and then checked in to their hotel, which Andy had booked ahead from Shimla.

Andy only had a couple of hotels on his list, but given the size of the town, he felt sure there were quite a few more that would have been operating thirty-five years earlier. Given its relative remoteness at that time, he was sure any foreign visitor would have been conspicuous. Hugh confirmed this view. They had seen no other white faces during their brief visit thirty-five years earlier. So they agreed it would be worthwhile enquiring through as many hotels as possible. Andy and Maruti would adopt the same approach as previously, but also ask at each hotel the names of other hotels where they might also enquire.

The hotel they had checked in to was relatively modern, but an older staff member could well have worked at another hotel thirty-five years earlier. There was one on duty. He was helpful in that he provided five additional hotel names and locations, but did not recognise either of the men in the photographs. It was a good start, however, and by the end of the afternoon, Andy and Maruti had visited four hotels, spoken to three older workers, and had a total of twelve hotels on their list. It was still daylight, and before dinner, they visited the ancient temple on the riverside of the highway and peered through the fence into the palace across the highway from the temple.

JOHN POLLARD

Hugh and Ruth wandered around town the next day, mainly window-shopping. They made a few purchases: some silk scarves to take home as gifts to family and friends and a nicely carved wooden elephant for their young granddaughter. Meanwhile, Andy and Maruti were busy visiting the hotels on their list. It was later that afternoon that the investigator struck a promising lead. One of the men interviewed thought he recognised the scar-faced man. He said that he was working at another Rampur hotel when a man came in looking for someone strong to help him. The scar-faced man promised to pay well. The Indian had asked his hotel manager for permission to assist the foreigner, but his request was refused, so he gave the man the name of a friend who was not at work that day and told him how to find him.

'Did your friend say anything about the job?'

'No. He did not say anything. When I asked him about the foreigner, he seemed very nervous and denied doing any work for him, but I think he was lying. Perhaps he was thinking that I wanted to share the money with him.'

'Where is your friend now?'

'He is not my friend now. After that time, we became less friendly. We speak if we meet in the street, but that is all.'

'That's sad. But do you know where he now lives?'

'It's a long time since I last saw him. I think he lives in a house near Nirath.'

'We would like to speak with him about the man with the scar. Can you tell us his name and how we can find him?'

'His name is Khushwant Singla. I think you must go to Nirath and ask there.'

Andy thanked the old man and gave him a generous tip. The man also willingly gave details as to where he might be contacted if Andy needed further help.

Over dinner that evening, they discussed the strategy they should adopt in Nirath. The fact that they only had a name but no photograph was likely to make the search rather difficult, and Andy was also concerned lest a group including Westerners might frighten their quarry away. Andy's plan, therefore, was that Maruti and Anupam make enquiries on his behalf whilst he and the others went off as tourists.

'What should our Indian colleagues do if they locate Singla?' asked Hugh.

'A very good question and one I've been pondering over all afternoon,' was Andy's response. 'We don't want him to flee and disappear without trace. Maruti and Anupam will have to handle this on the run. I definitely want to be present when he is shown the photos of Scarface and Dan, because I believe I can put more pressure on him and, if necessary, frighten him into answering our questions. I don't want him frightened before that. Maruti and Anupam will have to make the man as comfortable as possible in their company. Money is very useful as a bargaining tool, especially here in India. I think they have to tell the man they know someone who needs information and is prepared to pay very well for it—which is true. To show faith, I will give Maruti an envelope containing a generous sum, and when they give it to him, they can promise twice the amount again if he cooperates.

'I'd dearly like to get a photo of him in case we lose him and have to track him down again, but not at the price of scaring him away.'

Hugh's mind was racing. 'May I make a suggestion? I presume Maruti will be doing most of the talking. So why not find a small camera and give it to Anupam? He could perhaps wander off as if losing interest and subtly photograph the man from a distance. One can always enlarge the image.'

'That's a good idea. It might very well work. But the man must not know he is being photographed. I can't give either of my professional cameras to Anupam—they're too complicated, but I did bring a small tourist-type digital camera, so I'll give him that to use.'

'Any other suggestions?'

'I can't think of any.'

'I'll meet Maruti and Anupam at eight thirty in the morning and rehearse everything with them many times. They have to get it right. I suggest then that we set out for Nirath around 10:00 a.m.'

It was an excited team that set out the next morning for the short drive west to Nirath. The two Indians were obviously delighted to have been given so much responsibility and clearly appreciated the confidence Andy was showing in them. Whilst they were making enquiries, Ruth, Hugh, and Andy would explore the famous sun temple and anything else of interest in the village.

The three tourists were a little surprised when their guide and driver appeared at the sun temple earlier than expected. Maruti reported that they had started their enquiries at the western end of the village. They had approached each person they encountered and asked whether that person knew Khushwant Singla. Some simply said no and continued on their way. A couple of times, a small group had gathered around them. A middle-aged man in one of these groups said that he knew Khushwant Singla. He told them that Singla was an older man who had moved from the village about two years ago. He was not sure, but believed that Singla now lived near Jeori. The man seemed reliable and certain about the information he had provided. Andy thanked their Indian colleagues very warmly.

'If we don't have any success in Jeori, we can always return and continue our enquiries here. There must be others who know him.'

To reach Jeori, they had to go back through Rampur. So they stopped for lunch at the same roadside restaurant they had visited a few days earlier. The service was slower than they would have liked, and whilst they were waiting, they chatted away enthusiastically about the progress they seemed to be making.

'Have you told Mrs Blum about our progress to date?' asked Hugh.

'I try to keep her informed as frequently as possible. It depends on when and whether I have the opportunity to e-mail the office. Our secretary then phones her. The little feedback that I have received is that she is happy—even a little excited—by what we have achieved up to Shimla. I'm not sure that I can access the Internet in Rampur, so I may have to telephone instead.'

Jeori turned out to be somewhat larger than they had envisaged, with sizable military barracks nearby where soldiers trained for high-altitude mountain action. It was hard to know where to start looking. The nearest tourist attraction was the Bhimakali temple at Sarahan seventeen kilometres off the national road via a slow narrow winding road. Andy needed to be close at hand if and when Maruti and Anupam found Singla. He could not therefore go to Sarahan. Nor could Anupam spend the time driving the tourists there. They decided therefore to find a small restaurant where Andy could drink tea, update his report, and read, whilst Hugh and Ruth took a taxi to Sarahan. Maruti and Anupam would begin a methodical search for Singla.

Anupam found a suitable restaurant and the owner organised a taxi for Ruth and Hugh. Shortly after leaving the main road, they passed the military barracks and further along the road encountered a large number of soldiers marching up the steep hill carrying rifles with heavy rucksacks on their backs loaded with rocks. Soon they were out in the countryside winding up the mountainside through apple orchards. The scenery was splendid. Their driver had obviously taken many tourists to Sarahan and seemed to be well informed about the temple. They were in no hurry and wandered around at a leisurely pace taking many photographs. As a backdrop, the temple had snow-capped mountains only a few kilometres away. After they had finished exploring the temple, the taxi driver led them to the nearby Raja Palace, and they entered the garden to photograph the large house with dark ornate woodwork on the second storey and white lattice and some ornamentation around the ground floor veranda. The building looked more like a rather nice grand house than a palace.

They were in no hurry to get back to Jeori, and on the way down the mountainside, their driver stopped frequently so that they could take photographs, so it was relatively late in the afternoon when they rejoined Andy at the restaurant. They ordered some tea and cakes and waited for Maruti and Anupam.

Their Indian colleagues arrived just before 6:00 p.m. looking rather dejected and sadly announced that they had had no success. They had managed to make enquiries over only about a third of the town. Andy thanked them generously and did his best to cheer them up. 'We'll come back tomorrow early so that we have all day to search.'

Nevertheless it was a rather subdued, quiet journey back to Rampur.

There was little left for Hugh and Ruth to do in Jeori the next day, so with Andy's agreement, they remained in Rampur, out of the way. Andy managed to obtain a couple of paperbacks at the hotel so that he had enough to read and keep him occupied at the restaurant in Jeori whilst Maruti and Anupam continued their search.

Given their lack of success the previous afternoon, Andy was most surprised when mid morning, a very excited Maruti came running up to the table where he was reading. 'We've found him! I was speaking with a man who owns a restaurant and he told me that Khushwant Singla occasionally works for him in the kitchen. He described very carefully the house where Khushwant Singla lives and we have been there. We saw a man in the house, but we have not spoken with him. He looked like an old man. What should we do? Anupam is watching the house in case the man leaves.'

Andy could hardly believe his ears. 'Excellent. Where is the car?'

'The car is in the centre of town not far from here.'

'Okay. You go back to the house and keep watch. Send Anupam back to me. We'll come in the car and park a short distance from the house where we are not obvious. I'll remain in the car and watch whilst you and Anupam go to the house to speak with the man. Follow our original plan and bring him over to the car. If he is not cooperative, signal me and I'll come over.'

Fifteen minutes elapsed. Maruti and Anupam had changed places, and Andy was seated in the car about fifty yards from the house. Andy watched as the two Indians approached the door of the small dwelling. He saw the door open and a man come out. There was a short conversation and the man made negative gestures. Anupam started to wander off slowly whilst Maruti continued his conversation with the man. He saw Anupam raise the camera surreptitiously a couple of times to take photographs and then continue to stroll around nonchalantly. Maruti passed over the envelope full of rupees. The man opened it, and whilst Andy could not see his eyes, he imagined them to be gleaming with greed, because even as far away as fifty yards, the change in the man's body language was obvious. 'Aye, money speaks,' Andy muttered to himself.

The conversation outside the house continued for a couple more minutes and then the two men started to walk towards the car. Anupam turned and walked over to join them. When they got close to the car, Andy opened the door and got out. The Indian seemed taken aback almost immediately and halted. Perhaps his experience with an aggressive violent white man decades earlier made him apprehensive, so Andy called out, 'Please come over. You have nothing to fear if you help me. I won't harm you.'

Maruti obviously realised that the man did not understand Andy, so he translated Andy's message. The man relaxed a little, but still looked apprehensive.

'I will give you double that amount of money after you have given me the information I need, and then I will not trouble you again.'

The man still looked wary, but came over to the tall Scotsman. There was a pause whilst Andy reached into the car and took a folder out of his briefcase. He withdrew the photograph of Scarface and showed it to the nervous man. Andy did not need to say anything because the look of terror that immediately came over the man's face was sufficient to tell him that he recognised the face. Maruti asked him whether he recognised the face.

'He says he does not recognise the face, but I don't believe him.'

'Tell him that the man is a dangerous criminal and we want to see him punished. Tell him that if he helps us, he will not get into trouble.' Andy then produced the photograph of Dan. 'We only want to find the criminal and this man whom we believe was murdered by the criminal. I repeat. If you help us, you will not be harmed, and I will keep my promise to pay you twice what you have already been paid. If you don't help us, you won't get the additional money and we'll give the police your photograph and tell them about your involvement in the murder of the young man.'

Andy was not quite sure how he might convince the police, as his evidence was all circumstantial, even if his suppositions were correct and a murder did take place thirty-five years earlier. Maruti took a little while translating Andy's words, and as he spoke, it was clear that the man was wavering.

There was a long silence, and Andy asked Maruti to tell the frightened man once again that if he provided the information Andy wanted, the man would be unharmed and would get the generous reward. When Maruti had finished communicating this, the man rather hesitantly started telling his story.

# 12

# Singla's Story

SINGLA APPEARED TO accept the promise Andy and his Indian colleagues had made that if he cooperated he would be safe and would be rewarded. Or it may have been that he was worried about being handed over to the police as an accessory to murder. Either way, he began to give his account of what happened decades earlier, very slowly and hesitantly. Maruti translated.

'When I was a young man, I used to work at a hotel in Rampur doing many different jobs inside and outside the hotel. I was strong then. One day when I was not at work, another man who worked there sent me a message that an Englishman needed a strong assistant and that he would pay well. I badly needed money because my brother was very ill and my family could not afford to get medical attention for him. So I went immediately to the hotel to take the job.

'I waited for a short time and then the Englishman appeared. He told me that he needed help lifting something heavy and taking it somewhere. The way he behaved frightened me, and the big scar on his face made him seem even more terrifying. I didn't want to go with him, but it was too late to say no, and I needed the money so badly for my brother. So I went with him in his car.

'He told me that he wanted to bury something large where it would not be found, and he needed my help. He would pay me ten thousand rupees. I must never tell anyone about what I had done. Otherwise he would kill me.

'It was a lot of money and I agreed.

'He asked me to help find a suitable location. We spent a couple of hours looking for a suitable place. I suggested various possibilities, but none of these was acceptable to the Englishman.'

'So what did you do?' Andy asked through Maruti.

It was clear that Sangla understood some basic English, because he started to answer Andy's question before Maruti had time to translate it.

'The Englishman decided to look along the narrow road which runs from the edge of Rampur to Narkanda. There are many deep ravines at the side of this road and there is very little traffic. The Englishman got out of the car to look at several of the ravines and eventually selected one which was virtually inaccessible from the river below or from the road. I couldn't believe it when he told me to help him push the car and its contents over the edge—a perfectly good car! The man with the scar then told me that we must go down to the car which was now fifty metres below the road and barely visible. He insisted that I had to go down with him. I pointed out to him that the edge of the ravine was too steep and slippery, and we would need ropes. He had a closer look and seemed to agree with me.

'I said that if he gave me some money, I would walk back into Rampur and buy the rope. He refused. He said he would walk back with me. Perhaps he realised that I was very frightened and suspected that I might disappear. So we walked back together into Rampur, bought rope, and returned to the ravine.'

'Did anyone see you walking to Rampur, in the shop, and returning to the ravine?' asked Andy, again through Maruti.

'All the way into Rampur and back, I walked a respectful distance behind the Englishman. There was no one on the narrow Narkanda road. We passed a few people along the highway. They would have noticed that he was a foreigner, but I don't think they paid much attention to him. I showed him the store where he could buy the rope, and he gave me money to purchase it. He waited outside, making sure I did not escape. We then walked back to the ravine.'

'Okay. So you returned to the ravine. Please continue telling us what happened.'

'It was not easy getting down to the car, and it took about half an hour to reach it. We found it on its side. I was told to dig a large hole about five feet deep right next to the car. Fortunately the earth was damp and reasonably soft, and I completed the job in about three hours. The Englishman then told me to remove the contents of the car boot. It was then that I discovered that what he wanted to bury was a body. I shrunk back and refused to touch the body.

'The Englishman then took a gun from his bag and pointed it at me. I had no choice but to do what he ordered. I dragged the body out of the boot and pushed it into the ditch. I then refilled the ditch, and together we rolled the car over on to its roof so that it covered the area where the body was buried.'

'Thanks,' said Andy. 'Would you please show us the ravine where all this happened?'

'I have been suffering with this memory for so many years. It was difficult living so close to where it happened and re-living the nightmare every day, and my brother died anyway. A couple of years ago, I could not bear it anymore, so I decided to move to this house in Jeori. Many people in Rampur and Nirath wondered why all those years ago I changed so much so suddenly, but I could not tell them. Yes, I can show you the ravine, but I will not go down to the car.'

'Okay. That's been very helpful. Here is part of the reward I promised. I'll give you the rest when you have shown us the ravine and we have located the car. We will go back to Rampur tonight. Tomorrow morning I will send the car to collect you and bring you to Rampur so that you can show us the ravine and we can locate the car. Okay?'

'Yes.'

Although the man was still very tense and trembling with emotion, Andy gained the impression that he was relieved to have been able to tell his story for the first time and get it off his chest.

It had been a very successful day. Nevertheless, with Andy, Maruti, and Anupam all deep in thought about the frightened Indian's story, it was a quiet journey back to Rampur. At dinner that night, Hugh and Ruth were amazed when Andy recounted Singla's story.

Early the next morning, Anupam headed off to Jeori to collect Singla whilst Andy went shopping for rope and steel stakes. It was close to 10:30 a.m. when he and the three Indians headed to the western edge of Rampur, crossed the bridge over the Sutlej tributary, and turned left into the narrow back road towards Narkanda to locate the burial site. Singla sat in the front of the car with Anupam so that he could readily see and identify the ravine. They had only gone a short distance along the very narrow windy road when Singla started to look more intently at each steep precipice that dropped from the edge of the road down into the river valley below. The road was narrow with curve after curve for Anupam to negotiate, and they were forced to travel slowly, which meant it was easy for Anupam to stop when Singla pointed out the burial ravine. They got out of the car, and Anupam drove it a little further on to a slightly wider section of the road where he could park it safely. There was also the added advantage that a passer-by would be less likely to notice what was happening in the ravine and stop to investigate.

'Down there,' the nervous and frightened Indian pointed.

The ravine looked overgrown and very inaccessible. It seemed to drop away very steeply from the road, flattening out somewhat nearer to the river. Andy could not see the car, but that was hardly surprising. If Singla's description of its position as being about fifty metres down the slope were correct, the car wreck would have to lie on the steep slope of the ravine. There would still be further drop of around fifty metres to the flatter area near the river. Access to the car from the river would be more difficult than clambering down from the road.

Andy collected his recently purchased rope and stakes from the car and prepared to clamber down the slope. He certainly needed the rope to assist him down the first thirty metres. After that, trees that grew on the side of the ravine meant that he could dispense with the rope and slide from tree to tree. Coming back would be more difficult but not impossible. After about another thirty metres, he saw what he thought might be the car and slid down to where it lay.

It was indeed a car, very rusty, lying on its roof, and tightly packed in position with silt that had washed down the ravine over the decades. 'I think we have it!' he muttered to himself. 'Now I need help.' He photographed the scene and then began the difficult climb back up the ravine, crawling on all fours at times and slipping a lot. Once he reached the rope, he quickly abseiled to the top, where he showed the others his photographs of the car. Singla was interested even though it brought back the terrifying memories that still haunted him.

There was nothing else they could do at the site, so they returned to the hotel in Rampur. Whilst he had not actually confirmed the existence of a body at the site, Andy was convinced that Singla had been perfectly honest with him. He thanked him warmly again and paid him the remainder of his reward. He was rewarded by Singla's first smile and a nod of thanks. Anupam then drove him back home to Jeori.

Andy needed physical and forensic help. He could get the physical help locally, but that would quickly draw unwanted attention to the site. Forensic help could only be obtained from further afield and he needed advice from the office. It was the middle of the night in Buffalo, but he wanted advice as soon as possible. So he rang and left a fairly detailed report, hoping for a response that evening. It was another twenty-four hours, however, before he received a response, and it was good news.

His colleagues had contacted an investigation company in Mumbai and negotiated their assistance. A team comprising a forensic expert and two labourers would be on their way the following day and might be expected to begin excavating the site within about two days.

He told Hugh and Ruth the news at breakfast the next day. They were delighted, but wondered how an Indian private investigation team could investigate the site and possibly exhume a body at the site without official permission. Andy agreed that officially they should be informing the police. 'However, as long as the police don't become aware of our activities in the ravine, there shouldn't be any problem. They have thousands of other much-higher priorities. With a population of a billion, how many deaths do you think there are in India every year? Around five million. How many do you think are properly reported with medical certificates? Less than half. How many partially cremated bodies flow down the Ganges every year? Hundreds, possibly thousands. Some are also believed to be bodies thrown into the holy river by police to avoid having to make formal enquiries about suspicious deaths. How many deaths are homicides? Well over forty thousand. In spite of the peaceful image most Westerners have of India, it's quite a violent society. There are other important crimes which need their attention—for example, the hundreds of children kidnapped every year and never seen again by their parents.'

Andy sounded just a little defensive, but the point he was making was clear. Unless the police were forced to attend to the case, they would not really want to spend time investigating a thirty-five-year-old suspected murder of a foreigner by another foreigner. They had more than enough on their plate with more recent cases. 'The site is well hidden and we will be taking every precaution to ensure that no one finds out what we are doing. Of course, if there is a body and it turns out to be that of Mrs Blum's son, as we suspect, and she wants his remains returned to the United States, then at that stage we'll have to go through all the official channels.'

'How long will the investigations at the site take?' Hugh asked.

'It's very hard to say, but my guess is that it will probably take at least a week.'

'What do you suggest Ruth and I do?'

'I know you wanted to explore the region further into the Himalaya nearer Tibet. Why don't you take the opportunity now? A travel agent in Shimla can probably help, but as a start, why don't you ask the hotel reception?'

Hugh and Ruth did not need to be persuaded. On the way back from breakfast, they stopped by at reception. The young man on duty pulled out a rather battered book with handwritten addresses and telephone numbers. He did not know an appropriate travel agent in Shimla and suggested they telephone Cox and Kings, 'a very old and good travel agent' in Delhi, which should be able to help. He gave them the number and explained how they could dial it from their room.

# 13

# Forensic Assistance

HUGH TELEPHONED COX and Kings in Delhi as soon as they got back to their room and spoke with a helpful agent. Hugh explained what they wanted to do. The agent was clearly interested in their out-of-the-ordinary travel request and promised to fax a suggested itinerary and an estimated cost later in the day.

They were delighted when around three thirty in the afternoon, the receptionist called to announce the arrival of a fax from Delhi from Cox and Kings, 'the oldest travel agent in the world' established in 1758. The proposed seven-day itinerary would take them east from Rampur up the Sutlej to Sangla and on to Kalpa and Pooh. They would cross over the Sutlej near Khab and follow its major tributary, the Spiti, in a northerly direction. Sadly, Khab was the closest they would get to Shipki La (only about five kilometres away as the crow flies, but more than twenty on a zigzagging mule track). The mountainous border region was still restricted and would remain so as long as there were tensions between the two giant nations.

The route would then take them to Nako and Kaza and over the 4,550-metre Kunzum Pass on their way to Manali. From here, they would follow a road in a roughly southerly direction to Shimla and back to Rampur. The itinerary listed many significant Tibetan Buddhist temples they would visit and other important sites. There were also warnings that many of the roads were subject to landslides and the travel agent could not be held responsible for any delays and additional costs caused by landslides or unexpected snowfalls. They were also advised to take out special 'adventure insurance'.

Cox and Kings revealed that they did not themselves organise tours in this region but gave the business to a reputable travel agent in Shimla, and it was this agent who had designed the itinerary. The price quoted for a car, driver, and experienced guide seemed very reasonable. So they immediately telephoned the Cox and Kings agent in Delhi to thank him and accept the arrangement.

The next morning, they were driven back to Shimla by Anupam to meet the local travel agent, who told them that special passes were required to enter the Himalayan region near the Tibetan border, and these had to be obtained from the district magistrate's office. It would be a slow process and could take a whole day. So they checked in to their previous hotel and farewelled Anupam who returned to Rampur.

At ten the next morning, they met the local travel representative, and half an hour later, the tedious bureaucratic process began. They had to wander from one office to another in a couple of run-down buildings on the southern slope of the city. The young woman behind the desk at the main office seemed rather bored and uninterested and not a little irritated that she had to deal with a special out-of-the-usual complex process.

'The British taught the Indians bureaucracy, and the Indians seem to have perfected it to an art form,' was Hugh's wry comment as they sat patiently waiting to be called back to the counter. It was with some relief and considerable surprise that by mid afternoon, they had the necessary stamped papers with the district magistrate's signature. They were now ready to head up into the Himalaya towards Shipki La.

Their guide and driver arrived at their hotel the following morning at nine and introduced themselves. Raju, the guide, spoke almost flawless English, which, they learned a few days later, he had perfected by listening daily to BBC radio. He told the Australians that both his parents came from Nepal, and this seemed to explain his short stature, at least in Ruth's and Hugh's minds. Nadir, their driver, spoke only a few words, but had a continuous smile on his face. Both lived in Manali and loved the mountains. Both men were a delight to be with, and the tourists looked forward to their adventure with them.

Back in Rampur, Andy waited as patiently as he could for the forensic expert and his labourers. By the time they arrived, Hugh and Ruth were on their way east and well past Rampur.

Mr Bandopadhyay, the forensic expert, arrived from Mumbai in the late afternoon, and Andy spent a couple of hours giving him the background to the investigation. He then took him to the section of road overlooking the site so that he could assess what was needed. The man, who spoke excellent English with a heavy Indian lilt, did not seem fazed by the prospect of undertaking an unauthorised exhumation at an unofficial burial site. Andy asked about his assistants. It was immediately clear that they were from a lower caste. They had travelled separately from him and were staying elsewhere in town. They normally worked in the 'towers of silence' in Mumbai and had taken leave to assist in the exhumation. They would find their own way to the site the next morning. Mr Bandopadhyay would tell them where they had to go.

Two simply dressed men were there waiting for them when Andy and the Mumbai expert arrived at the site the next morning. Andy led the way down the steep slope using his rope, followed by the forensic expert and then by the two assistants with shovels. After some discussion, the men began digging the silt from around the outside of the car. The soil was not particularly difficult to remove. The silt that had been deposited inside the wreck was more awkward, and there was no way the car could be moved until that soil was taken out and placed well away from the car. It would take some time. So Andy left the three Mumbai men at work and returned to the hotel in Rampur.

It was late that afternoon when the Mumbai expert called Andy from the hotel reception and reported that all the silt had been removed from the car and its surrounds and that the next morning they hoped to roll the car over onto its side and start excavating the presumed burial site.

When they arrived at the site the next morning, the two labourers were already trying to roll the car onto its side, but were finding the task very difficult because the slope meant that they had to raise the centre of gravity of the wreck. Trying to roll it onto its other side was no better. The three from Mumbai discussed at length what to do. Mr Bandopadhyay then outlined the conclusion they had come to. They would need a jack, two crowbars, and some timber to support the car as they slowly raised one side. For the moment, they could do nothing more.

They were fortunate that the road above the site was little used, and as far as they could tell, their activities in the ravine had attracted no attention. Andy was determined to keep it that way. He was concerned lest his continued presence in the town and purchases aroused curiosity. He therefore instructed Anupam to shop in Narkanda rather than Rampur for the necessary tools and timber. Transporting the timber would be a problem because the car had only a small roof rack and the timber would be quite heavy. Anupam would probably have to make a couple of journeys.

With no action likely at the site for several hours and, when work resumed, rolling the car onto its side likely to take some time, Andy had Anupam drop him off at his hotel. He felt certain that within a day or so, Dan Blum's remains would be revealed. Their forensic examination would take rather longer. All the evidence pointed to Scarface as the killer. So back at the hotel, he faxed his Buffalo office, briefly reporting progress and, temporarily forgetting that he himself had previously unsuccessfully requested an update on George William's whereabouts from the London investigation company, asked his colleagues to make enquiries through that group.

It was only when he received the response from his colleague at Buffalo that he remembered with some embarrassment his earlier London enquiry.

*Our London contacts have just informed us that without additional information, they cannot help us. They said they have already told you this. It seems that when they started putting all their files on computer some years back, the decision was made to cull all the ancient files which had been closed for more than five years. All they recorded was the name and contact details of the client and the date the case had been closed. It would seem, therefore, that the family retaining the London people had eventually lost interest in tracking Patrick O'Connell. Any suggestions?*

Andy put the fax in his briefcase to mull over.

Meanwhile, the Mumbai team continued with their task. Rolling the car onto its side and propping it up safely took a whole day even with the equipment purchased in Narkanda. They dug down about a metre and a half before uncovering evidence of a body. After this, it was painstaking work removing soil without disturbing the remains so that the forensic man could take photographs and note anything that might be important. He then began examining the remains themselves, trying to disturb the body as little as possible while at the same time searching for organic material that could be used to identify the deceased using DNA techniques. There was a bullet hole in the front of the skull—very likely the cause of death. The man must have been shot at least twice, because there was a bullet lodged in the spine, which the forensic expert carefully removed.

The Mumbai man reported back to Andy every evening. When he was satisfied he had all that he could reasonably expect, he suggested that the grave could now be refilled and the car rolled back on its roof in its former position. Whilst this was easier than raising it, it still took more than a day because they had to make sure that when they had finished, there would be minimal evidence of their activities.

Ruth and Hugh arrived back in Rampur a day after the grave had been returned to its previous condition and the car refilled with silt. Andy had farewelled the Mumbai team the previous afternoon and they were on their way back south. He was clearly very excited when he revealed what the team had achieved. 'Now we can go home and wait for the detailed report from Mumbai.'

It was almost as an afterthought that he remembered to ask the Australians about their adventure.

'We had a great time, but let's meet for dinner and we can tell you all about it then.'

It was a very relaxed and rather excited trio that sat down to dinner that evening and exchanged stories, but as the evening went on, their mood became more subdued with the realisation that their time in the Himalaya was now almost over.

Hugh recounted their drive up river towards the Tibetan frontier along narrow gravel roads with sheer drops of many hundreds of metres and no guard rails. Meeting an oncoming truck was very challenging, particularly when their car was on the outer side of the road and had to back to the very edge of the precipice to allow the truck through. Just a small nudge from a truck could send them flying into oblivion. Ruth revealed that she had been terrified at the outset, but became 'a little more relaxed' as her confidence in their careful driver increased. Every time he saw an approaching vehicle, he would fold back his wing mirror and slow to a crawl. The biggest sheer drop they passed was on the old road built in British times on the northern side of the river near Kalpa with a nine-hundred-metre precipice. There were tyre tracks only six inches from the crumbling unfenced edge of the road. No longer the main road to the frontier, it was still the only access road to a number of local villages, and their guide took them there in the car simply to see the drop.

Sadly their hope of reaching the Tibetan frontier had once again been thwarted. They met the Shipki La turnoff a short distance before Khab, but the final section of road was still out of bounds. They had walked a short distance along the riverside track from where they could just see part of the onward Shipki La track as it zigzagged up the bare rocky mountain, but that was all. Nevertheless, they were much closer than they had been in 1968.

The bare, dry, rugged rocky cliffs with snow-capped peaks high above continued as they followed the road along the Spiti River in a northerly direction. Shear drops of hundreds of metres from the unguarded edge of the road and hairpin bends made the onward journey just as exciting as the earlier one along the Sutlej. In places, the road was simply carved out of the mountain as a tunnel, except that the tunnel was open on one side and there was a precipice dropping straight down to the rushing river below.

The Tibetan-style Buddhist monasteries they had visited in Nako, Tabo, and Lalung dated from around AD 1,000, and they were delighted when the bespectacled tall monk at Lalung invited them to drink tea with him. They were surprised to see a health poster in English on the wall instructing readers to wash their hands. Along the way, they visited a number of other ancient remote monasteries.

Near a village named Ki, they saw first-hand how villagers from remote communities manage to reach more accessible towns. Rather than walk for days along tracks that go down and up the steep sides of rugged ravines, they take a shortcut over the ravine in a basket on a cable. Hugh filmed three men doing this, standing in a tiny basket as it was hauled across the wide deep ravine by a person on the far side using a rope. There was no way Ruth and Hugh would be game enough to take the 'flight' over the ravine, which was hundreds of metres wide and equally deep. The locals, however, did not seem concerned. The Australians' guide told them that he and their driver had both crossed ravines in the Himalaya in this manner.

Further on near Langza at around four thousand metres, they were taken to a remote area famous for fossils. Their guide and driver set out to uncover a fossil for them whilst they walked on to the nearby village. Their companions did not find anything for them, but a small broken fossil caught Hugh's eye as they strolled along the road. It was hard to believe the creature had been alive in the sea 70 million years earlier, before the Indian subcontinent began climbing over Asia to form the mighty Himalaya.

The stark rocky surroundings continued for much of the journey, but the scenery changed abruptly after they crossed the 4,550-metre Kunzum Pass and the 3,975-metre Rohtang Pass. Suddenly everything was lush and green. From here, they descended into Manali where they stayed overnight and visited a palace and several temples before travelling south to Shimla and back to Rampur.

JOHN POLLARD

Andy was obviously glad that his friends had had such an interesting and enjoyable adventure and seemed intrigued by their journey. They confessed, however, that they were a little disappointed that the whole area was now much more developed compared with what it must have been in 1968 and that there was a lot of evidence along the Sutlej of huge hydroelectric schemes being developed. 'Perhaps also it was the fact that we encountered a few tourists along the way—something we are not used to when we make such journeys.'

After dinner, Andy telephoned New Delhi to arrange their flights home two days later. Anupam would drive them back to the capital in the morning and they would have a rest day before flying out.

Andy spent most of the 'rest day' in Delhi writing up his full report. Hugh and Ruth simply relaxed by the pool. After the cooler, drier climate of the Himalaya region, it seemed simply too hot and humid to do much else.

The three met for dinner in the hotel restaurant that night and chatted about what they would be doing next week. Inevitably the conversation turned to the case that had brought them together and led to their friendship. 'Hopefully the laboratory in Mumbai will be able to extract some useful DNA. According to my colleagues, they have a good reputation. We'll then have to compare it with Mrs Blum's. If there is a match, then I'll try to track down Scarface. Bringing him to justice, however, will be rather more difficult. Officials in India and possibly elsewhere will have to be brought in, and they won't like what we've been doing! But that's another day!'

'How will Mrs Blum handle this?' asked Ruth.

'By now, I think, she realises that her son must be dead, and she wants to find out how he died, and if it was foul play, who murdered him. Obviously the details we will have to go through with her will be upsetting, but at least in the end, the mystery of his disappearance will be solved and that's what she really wants before she dies.'

Andy had a very early flight the next morning and would have to leave the hotel well before breakfast time. So they said their farewells at the restaurant and promised to keep in contact.

# 14

# Thai Holiday

RUTH AND HUGH had been home in Sydney for about a month when they received a telephone call from Andy. By then they were well settled into their usual routine. They had told their family about their Indian Himalayan adventure but had said little about the associated private investigation activities. They noticed that even over the few weeks they were away, their young granddaughter seemed to have grown and developed a lot.

Andy reported that he had gone personally to see Mrs Blum and reported their discovery. The Mumbai investigator had e-mailed Andy a photograph of the watch found on the exhumed body, and whilst Mrs Blum was not completely sure, she thought it was the one she and her husband had given Dan when he graduated from college. The meeting was obviously upsetting for her, but she thanked Andy warmly, and she readily agreed to provide a swab for DNA testing purposes.

Back in Mumbai, the forensic team had managed to obtain DNA from the material collected from the body. Whilst it was not perfect, the comparison with Mrs Blum's DNA was such that they were reasonably certain the body was indeed that of her missing son.

'I had some difficulty tracking down Scarface, but we seem to have found him in Bangkok. We made enquiries through the London investigation company, but they had destroyed their very old files on closed cases when they computerised everything some years back and the file on Scarface was obviously one of these. They kept a record of past clients, their contact details at the time the case was closed, and the date of closure, but that was all.

'We didn't know the name of the family tracking him, so we couldn't even tell them which record to open. However, a search of newspaper reports of the fatal armed robbery eventually revealed the name of the victim, and with this information, the London people were able to find their brief record. As might be expected, the contact details were out of date, but after some enquiries, they managed to find the family, who recalled that the last-known location they had for Patrick O'Connell from the investigators was Bangkok.

'I contacted our associated company in Bangkok by e-mail. We were lucky. After only twenty-four hours, they got back to us. George Williams is a well-known bar owner in the Bangkok red-light area. He owns a flourishing establishment named Barbies Bar, commonly referred to locally as Boobies Bar, and has been investigated a couple of times for providing underage prostitution. For reasons not entirely clear, no charges were ever laid. It seems he is still in Bangkok.

'I'm booked to fly to Bangkok in a week's time, where I hope to locate our suspect.

'Mrs Blum is very thankful for your invaluable help and would like to reward you with a holiday at her expense in Thailand. What she proposes is that you meet me in Bangkok, have a short spell there before flying north to Chiang Mai. She suggests that you might also like to relax in the sun in Phuket on the way home to Sydney. What do you say? Have you been to these places?'

'That's very generous of Mrs Blum. We visited Phuket and Bangkok in 1999 when we were driving to London. We spent a week in Phuket, but didn't spend any time in Bangkok. Driving through the capital was a real challenge! Ruth drove whilst I navigated. We haven't been to Chiang Mai, and we'd certainly like to go there. I think we'd like to accept the whole offer!'

'Well then, that's settled. I'll arrange your air tickets from this end. Okay?'

They agreed on a departure date.

When Hugh got off the telephone, Ruth immediately questioned Hugh's positive response. 'Do you think we should really be going to Bangkok with a private investigator who expects to track down a violent murderer there? You didn't ask me for my view.'

'Sorry. I just thought you would like to accept a generous free holiday in Thailand. Should I ring Andy back and decline Mrs Blum's offer?'

'No, but I think at least you could have asked me and we should have given safety some consideration. I want to see our granddaughter grow up and hopefully see some more grandchildren.'

Hugh felt suitably reprimanded, and they discussed the holiday for half an hour. Eventually they agreed they were happy to accept the holiday. As Hugh pointed out, 'We'll be in Bangkok and see Andy from time to time, but we won't be accompanying him when he seeks out Scarface.'

Two days later, open-dated return tickets arrived in the mail from the Sydney office of Thai Airways.

Their plane touched down in Bangkok the following Thursday evening. After the usual formalities, they took a taxi downtown and checked in to their hotel. At reception, they were handed an envelope containing a handwritten message from Andy:

*Hope your flight was comfortable. See you for breakfast downstairs around 8:30? Okay? I'm in room 809. Best regards, Andy.*

Their hotel room was spacious, and a welcoming message from the hotel manager accompanied a generous bowl of tropical fruit. After the ten-hour flight from Sydney and the muggy heat of Bangkok, they were pleased to shower and retire early.

Their wake-up call came through at seven forty-five, and by eight thirty, they were down in the restaurant. Andy was obviously pleased to see them, and they were delighted to be in his company again. It seemed like only yesterday that they were together. The waiter brought them tea and coffee before they started tackling the generous buffet breakfast. After a few minutes of general conversation, Andy brought them up to date on his activities. He gave a more detailed account of the investigations his firm had undertaken leading to the location of Scarface in Bangkok. As he had told them previously by telephone, Mrs Blum was very appreciative of their help and was delighted that they had accepted her invitation to holiday in Thailand.

Andy reported that he had arrived a few days earlier. On Wednesday evening, he had taken a taxi to the Nana Plaza where he found Barbies Bar and spent a couple of hours enquiring about Scarface and observing the action. 'My visit didn't bear fruit, and I plan to return there tonight. The beers were expensive, but worse were the drinks I felt obliged to purchase for the girls who joined me at my table and then offered to come back to my hotel with me.'

'Were you tempted?' asked Hugh with a smile.

'Of course! They were all attractive young girls—but I kept my mind on the case. I asked each of the girls about Mr George Williams. They all denied knowing him, and my impression was that they were probably

JOHN POLLARD

genuine. I walked over to the bar and spoke to two of the barmen. They both denied knowing him. They were not interested in talking, and the noise and constant interruptions when I tried to converse with them made it difficult to judge whether they were hiding anything. My guess is that as staff they would have to know him. Whether they heard me correctly or were trying to protect him was impossible to tell with all the noise. Maybe that was the problem with the girls too. I didn't really get the opportunity to show anyone a photo of Scarface.

'By this stage, the bar was very busy. An older Japanese man left hand in hand with a pretty young girl, and I rushed over to take possession of their table. Then, for about an hour, I sat drinking beer, bought a few more very expensive lady drinks, and declined some very tempting offers. Around 11:30 p.m., I left, found a taxi, and returned here. That's my story—and I'm sticking to it!' He finished with a smile.

'You plan to return tonight then?'

'Aye, and as many nights as it takes. If those lads at the bar understood me, and know George Williams, they will have reported back to him, and I might see him sooner rather than later. Who knows?

'Why don't you two make the most of Mrs Blum's generosity and become tourists for the day. I've got a few things to attend to, but I'd appreciate it if we could meet for dinner—I hate dining alone if I can avoid it—but we'd have to eat reasonably early if I'm to visit Barbies Bar again tonight. I know Bangkok quite well. I'm sure I can find a good and interesting restaurant.'

Ruth and Hugh now regarded the tall muscular Scot as a good friend, and they willingly agreed to meet in the lobby around 6:00 p.m.

Various tours were available from the travel desk at the hotel. They definitely wanted to visit the ancient Thai capital Ayuthaya, but the tour was too long and they had only a few hours that day. It would be better to make that excursion later in their holiday, possibly on their way to Chiang Mai. So they chose a local city tour, visiting four of the most significant Bangkok tourist sights. It started with the Grand Palace, where they spent more than an hour and a half. Built in the late eighteenth century and home to the kings of Thailand for a hundred and fifty years, it turned out to be more than simply a palace, rather a whole complex of buildings, all exquisitely designed and built in characteristic Thai fashion. No longer the king's residence, the buildings are used for a variety of civic functions. The complex includes a temple that houses the much-revered fourteenth-century Emerald Buddha.

After a green curry chicken lunch at a simple restaurant, they were taken to the temple of the reclining Buddha forty-five metres long, with feet three metres long decorated in mother-of-pearl. Hugh immediately recalled it from a brief visit many years earlier with a Thai colleague. The other two sites included on the tour that afternoon were both temples— the beautiful 'marble temple' built at the turn of the twentieth century in Italian marble during the time of the great reformer King Chulalongkorn, whose ashes are buried beneath the Buddha statue, and Wat Traimit, home to the world's largest gold seated Buddha. Hugh and Ruth found the story behind this five-metre-high five-tonne figure interesting. Originally covered completely by plaster, the solid gold figure was only discovered when the Buddha was accidentally dropped as it was being moved. It seems that it was not unknown for precious gold Buddhas to be encased in plaster to avoid being plundered.

That evening they dined in a very relaxed atmosphere at a riverside fish restaurant. The conversation returned to Barbies Bar and Andy's plans for the evening. Hugh and Ruth were intrigued by the bar and its environment and asked Andy a lot of questions.

'Why don't you come along with me tonight?'

'No!' was Ruth's immediate response.

'I wasn't suggesting you should come. I don't think it would be appropriate. I really meant Hugh.'

'The answer's still no,' was Ruth's retort. Hugh wisely nodded his agreement.

On their way back to the hotel in the taxi, Ruth reflected on the conversation. Andy was a good friend and would probably appreciate Hugh's company whilst he sat in the bar hoping to make contact with George Williams. She trusted Hugh completely and felt sure the two men would be safe drinking their beers together. When they stepped out of the taxi and were entering the hotel lobby, she nervously remarked to Hugh, 'Why don't you go with Andy tonight? But I expect you back before midnight!'

'Are you sure?'

'Yes. I know you'll be good and I know Andy would appreciate the company. I'll watch TV and look forward to your return.'

Hugh was definitely curious and keen to check out the bar, so he told Andy Ruth's change in attitude, and a few minutes later, the two men hopped into a taxi and asked to be taken to Barbies Bar. As they moved off, the driver confirmed their destination with a knowing look in his rear

JOHN POLLARD

vision mirror, 'Boobies—yes?' and after a nod from Andy, they were on their way.

They got out of the taxi near the square and strolled around, Andy pointing out many features: bars full of foreign men mingling with beautiful young Thai women, hotels where rooms were let on an hourly basis. It was a completely new experience for Hugh. Twenty minutes later, they entered Barbies Bar and found a table.

It was immediately obvious why the bar had acquired the local name 'Boobies'. Under the 'Barbies Bar' sign outside were two neon Barbie dolls with exaggerated illuminated breasts, and inside the bar, the walls were plastered with suggestive girly pictures.

They ordered some cold Singha beers and surveyed the scene. Apart from the pictures on the walls, the décor was Spartan.

The bar was filling up, and it was not long before two attractive girls approached their table. The prettier one addressed Hugh.

'Hello, mister. Where you come from?'

Feeling awkward and somewhat embarrassed, he responded, 'Australia.'

The girls sat down. Hugh felt nervous and waited for the more experienced Andy to react. The latter eventually acquiesced to buying them drinks. The nearer girl moved closer to Hugh and placed her hand on his knee. The other girl plied her charms on Andy, who eventually, much to Hugh's relief, pushed her gently aside and told them, 'Sorry, ladies. No. Maybe another time. We are looking for a man called George Williams. Do you know him?'

The girls seemed surprised. 'Why you here?'

'We want to meet a man called George Williams.'

'Who?'

'George Williams.'

'No know Mister George.'

The girls left and were soon in the company of a couple of Germans at a nearby table. Andy ordered a second round of beers. An hour dragged by. Hugh continued to look around the bar and observed men buying girls drinks and leaving with them soon after. He noticed a very pretty girl entering and he was sure he had seen her leaving with an older man only about an hour earlier.

Andy broke the silence. 'I think it's time for me to talk to the lads at the bar again. You'll be okay waiting here?'

Hugh was not sure, but he answered, 'Yes.'

He started another beer and watched Andy. He could see Andy's problem in trying to speak with the men behind the bar. They were very busy and brushed him aside many times. But he remained persistent. Hugh was so busy watching Andy that he did not notice a very beautiful immaculately groomed girl approach, and he only became conscious of her when she sat down close beside him and placed her hand on his knee.

'Hello, mister. Your friend no like girls? You no like girls? You like me? You buy me drink?' Her broken English with a Thai accent was husky and sexy.

'You're beautiful. I'll buy you a drink,' was Hugh's rather nervous reply. He wished he still had Andy with him.

Neither of them spoke. Hugh looked at the seemingly remote Andy and prayed for his return. His new companion moved her hand higher up between his thighs. This was a new experience and he did not know how to handle it. He didn't want to offend the girl and the sensation was not unpleasant. He just wished Andy would admit defeat at the bar and return to save him.

'Your friend no come back. Why you not come with me? I make you very happy.'

He looked in Andy's direction and almost sighed with relief when he saw him returning. He gently pushed the girl's hand away from his thigh and greeted his friend. Andy looked at him quizzically as the girl got up and departed. 'How do you like your kathoey?'

'My what?'

'How do you like your kathoey—your ladyboy, the transsexual?'

Hugh flushed with embarrassment. He had first heard of ladyboys as a young man forty years earlier when taken for a tour of Bombay at night and billy boys were pointed out to him. But he had never encountered one and certainly never had one place his/her hand between his thighs.

'That beautiful girl was a ladyboy?'

'Yes. There are many in Thailand—there are probably more here than anywhere else in the world. They even have their own special annual beauty pageant. With hormone treatment, they often develop breasts larger than the typical Thai woman. Some resort to breast implants. Very often they still have all their male equipment down below as well as breasts—that's probably true of the ones here. Of course others have had the full sex-change operation.'

Hugh was intrigued. They looked around, and Andy discretely indicated two others.

'How do you distinguish them?'

'Usually it is not too difficult. They tend to be taller than the girls and their breasts are often larger. They pay a lot of attention to their appearance and generally wear rather more make-up. Sometimes their Adam's apple gives them away, although they may try to hide this by wearing something around their neck. They also walk in a more exaggerated feminine manner.'

'How do you know so much about them?'

'I think I told you earlier that I'm divorced. I met my ex-wife here in Bangkok when I was on rec leave from the SAS and I later married her here. After my discharge from the SAS, we returned to Bangkok and lived here for a year. So I know this city and Thailand quite well. Incidentally, I also speak Thai reasonably fluently, but I'm keeping that fact under wraps during the investigation in case it turns out to be helpful.'

They were about to order another round of beers when two aggressive men strode up to the table and announced, 'Boss wants see you.'

Andy was not accustomed to being pushed around. 'He's not very polite. Why didn't he come to say hello himself?'

'Boss wants speak to you. Come!'

Both the 'heavies' standing over them put their hands in their pockets, and it appeared that they probably had concealed weapons.

'Okay', conceded Andy, 'but my friend has nothing to do with this. Leave him here.'

'Both come!'

Andy and Hugh tried not to look too meek as they were escorted across the noisy room and along a small corridor behind the main bar counter. A couple of patrons watched them with mild curiosity as they passed and then turned their attention back to their girls. Hugh now wished he had stayed back at the hotel with Ruth.

They were shown into a small office, where 'the boss' sat behind a large desk. It was immediately obvious he was not Scarface—unless he had had some remarkable plastic surgery. As soon as he spoke, it was even clearer that he was not their man, as he had a pronounced American accent. 'What do you two guys want? You are clearly not interested in the girls and you can get cheaper beer elsewhere, even at your hotel. What do you want? Are you trying to make trouble? Why do you keep coming here?'

The barmen had obviously told their boss about Andy's visits and the questions he was asking. The boss nodded to the two heavies, who frisked Andy and Hugh. They found no weapons, but took their wallets and passports, presumably to check their identities. The boss repeated his question. 'What do you guys want?'

'I'm looking for George Williams, who I believe is the owner of this bar and another bar in Pattaya. It is part of an international murder investigation.'

At the mention of the word 'murder', the man's face froze momentarily but soon regained his arrogant composure. 'I don't know anything about a murder. All I know is that George sold me his business here and the other at Pattaya a few weeks ago and told me that he intended migrating to Australia. I haven't seen him since.'

He was about to continue when pandemonium suddenly broke out in the bar. Men were shouting and girls screaming. There were sounds of tables and chairs being knocked over as customers rushed to escape. 'Shit—police!' The two heavies immediately hid their weapons in a desk drawer, and the three men stood trying to look nonchalant.

Now that the men's weapons were out of the way, Hugh and Andy both thought of making a dash out of the room, but there was no time, because within seconds, two policemen rushed in and indicated that they should stand still and not move. The police spoke to them in Thai, produced handcuffs, and shortly afterwards, bundled Andy and Hugh into a police paddy wagon. The boss and his heavies were bundled into another. As they awaited transportation to the police station, Hugh and Andy could still hear the sounds of foreign men arguing their innocence and demanding to be allowed to leave.

A quarter of an hour later, the paddy wagon started moving, and after a journey of only a few minutes, they arrived at the local police station, where they were dragged roughly out of the vehicle and given a thorough body search. In broken English, the police demanded their passports and Andy explained in English that the three men from the bar had taken them. It took a while for the officers to comprehend. Eventually they did, and Andy and Hugh were locked up, presumably for the night. Their protestations were completely ignored. At least they were in the same cell together and alone. The other three were presumably elsewhere.

There were two not very clean mattresses down one end of their cell and a rather dirty squat toilet at the other, with a tap alongside. 'I think we're here for the night,' was Andy's first comment when they were alone. 'I heard them say something in Thai about an officer who speaks English coming in the morning.'

'What do you think will happen then? Will we simply be let off with a warning about frequenting such a place?'

'Hard to know. We certainly haven't broken any law. I suspect it may depend on what the others say to our captors. We'll have to wait and see.'

It was a long uncomfortable, noisy, and largely sleepless night for both of them. They were roused from their mattresses by an unfriendly guard who presented them with cold food for breakfast, which they ate with difficulty. They both felt uncomfortable with the lack of privacy.

The policeman who spoke English arrived a couple of hours later. 'Why you try extort money from Mister Robinson?'

'Mr who?'

'Mister Robinson.'

'Who is Mr Robinson?'

'Mister Robinson own Boobies Bar.'

'I did not try to extort money from him.'

'Mister Robinson say you demand money. He good businessman.'

Andy responded slowly and firmly. 'I did not try to extort money from Mr Robinson. I came to find Mr George Williams.'

'Mister Williams gone. He sold bar to Mister Robinson. Why you demand money from Mr Robinson?'

'I want to speak with Mr Robinson.'

'Mister Robinson not here. He good businessman. He gone to Boobies Bar.'

It was clear that they were getting nowhere. Their interrogator also seemed to realise that he was getting nowhere and departed. Left again with nothing to read or watch, all the two prisoners could do was converse. First and foremost in their thoughts was their predicament. They conjectured about Mr Robinson and his henchmen. It seemed to both of them that the American had some sort of arrangement with one or more of the local police. The fact that police raids seemed to be a regular occurrence yet Robinson was allowed to return immediately and continue business suggested corruption, although they had no real evidence. George Williams's sudden disappearance was a mystery, and during their short encounter with the boss, Robinson had not volunteered any convincing explanation for the abrupt change in ownership of the two bars.

'Do you think there could have been some foul play?' Hugh asked.

'The thought had crossed my mind, but there is nothing really to substantiate it. It could well be that he did in fact leave to settle in

Australia. If so, the Australian immigration authorities would know. But we've got no way of finding out, especially in here!'

Hugh was concerned about Ruth, alone in Bangkok and worrying about his safety. At the same time, any enquiries she made might well expedite their release.

The conversation petered out after a while, and they lay on their dirty mattresses, silent and bored. Lunch was an improvement on breakfast—at least it was warm and more inviting. Given the toileting arrangements and the lack of privacy, Hugh prayed the food and water they were given would not cause them to go down with diarrhoea.

They did not speak during the meal and for a while afterwards. Eventually, however, the silence and boredom got to them and they started talking again.

'Tell me a little about your life, Hugh. Of course, I already know you like making major international motor vehicle journeys. But what about other interests, what you did during your working life and your family? Please don't think I'm prying. But I believe we have all become firm friends, and I'm happy to tell you more about myself when you've finished! I fear we have plenty of time.'

Hugh told Andy that he was born into a large close academic family. After completing a science degree majoring in mathematics, he won a scholarship to study in the United Kingdom towards a PhD degree. Six months after he arrived in England, he met Ruth in London where she was training as a nurse. They were married three years later as soon as he had completed his degree. His research had attracted the attention of scholars in the USA and was invited to spend a post-doctoral year at the University of Chicago. It was after this they made their 1968 overland journey to India. For the next thirty-three years, he had worked as an academic in Sydney. He had travelled a lot to academic meetings in the Americas, Europe, and Africa, as well as Australia and New Zealand, and published about eighty papers. Apart from his academic work, he had also advised some major companies and served on a major Australian government enquiry. He retired at 60 just a year ago to have more time for his other interests.

'And your family?'

'We have four children, two of whom are married, and one infant granddaughter. Three of our children live in Sydney, including our son with the granddaughter. The other married daughter lives in Europe.

We're a close family. We speak with our European daughter every week on the phone.'

'What about the other interests you mentioned?'

'Although I was an academic mathematician, I like gadgets and making things. I'm a bit of a handyman—and quite good at it, if I can be a little immodest! I've actually made some major additions to our house in Sydney and built our holiday house in the Blue Mountains. Such activities, unfortunately, are not kind to hands, and my playing of the pipe organ has suffered badly. I love classical music and our radio is permanently tuned to the relevant station. I am also a director of a charity and sing in our very active church choir. But that's enough about me. What about you?'

'Thanks. I am one of two boys. My dad—now retired—was a schoolteacher in Edinburgh who taught history. My mum worked as a bank teller. As you no doubt know, Scotland has its own very strong education system, and I was encouraged to study hard as well as play hard on the sporting field. I kept very fit and played in the top school team in each sport. My parents were pleased when I completed my final SCE Higher Grade examinations and looked forward to me going to university. I was happy with what I had achieved academically, but wanted a more physical career, and with somewhat reluctant support from my parents, I joined the army and later transferred to the Scots Guards. I enjoyed the life and, a few years down the track, received my commission.

'I was about halfway through by second six-year term with the Guards when I began to think about a change. I was still enjoying the life, but I also wanted a fresh challenge. So I applied to join the Special Air Service—or SAS as it's known in Britain. I made sure I was in peak condition before I undertook the selection tests, which are notoriously demanding physically.

'Most recruits come from the RAF, with smaller numbers from the other defence forces. The physical demands placed on applicants over several weeks are enormous, and the failure rate is very high, so I was extremely pleased when I learned that I had been successful.

'During some rec leave from the SAS, I travelled to the Far East, visiting Hong Kong, Singapore, and Bangkok. It was at this stage that I met my future wife. We kept in contact over two long years and she visited me a couple of times in Britain. Married life would be difficult with me in the SAS. So after a lot of soul-searching, I resigned, and we were married six months later. I had enjoyed my visits to the Far East, and we spent the first year of our married life in Bangkok. Fortunately, as a bachelor, I'd built up a reasonable bank balance over my years in the forces and I did not need to work at that time, although I did a few odd jobs related to security. Ultimately, of course, I had to find a proper paying job. So we returned to England, where I joined the police and, a couple of years later, started working in the private investigation industry.

'I think I already told you I'm divorced. Back in England, I used to keep in contact with some of the lads from the SAS. My wife went off with one of them. It was a very bitter experience.'

There was silence for a little while. Hugh broke it. 'You mentioned the very tough selection process for the SAS. What was involved?'

'You first have to sign a document certifying that you are prepared to accept arduous duties. Next comes the medical and battle fitness test. Then comes the difficult part. Each day, the soldier has to find his way from one point to another carrying full heavy army equipment. The terrain is very difficult, and the distance is increased each day. This continues for three weeks. At rendezvous points, you are given special intricate tasks to perform—for example, dismantling and reassembling an unfamiliar weapon—all this on four hours' sleep a night.

'After this comes Test Week, daily sixteen-mile marches carrying a thirty-kilogram pack and map-reading. Finally there is the Long Drag, a forty-mile march, which must be completed in twenty hours.

'So much for the testing process and the elimination of many applicants. Training follows: jungle training and survival, comprehensive first aid, escape and evasion, resistance to interrogation, and finally parachute training—in full kit. Those who survive the selection and training are then badged SAS soldiers.'

'What about your family?' Hugh asked.

'My parents are both retired, and I see them whenever I'm back in Scotland, which is not so often nowadays. My brother lives in Manchester and it is several years since I saw him. Sadly we seem to have gone our separate ways. As boys we were quite close.'

The afternoon passed slowly, and after a small warm Thai meal, they settled down for another long night on their mattresses. It was difficult to sleep in the non-air-conditioned cell with sporadic loud noises from adjacent cells and continuous street sounds.

# 15

# A Very Long Weekend

RUTH RETURNED TO their room feeling rather lonely and a little sorry she had encouraged Hugh to go with Andy. She turned on the television and flicked through the channels. Everything seemed to be in Thai. There were not even any American films with Thai subtitles. So she turned to CNN and watched it for a while, until the items started to become repetitive. She wished Hugh was with her.

She took a long shower, put on her nightie, and climbed into bed to read. It was hard to concentrate, and she looked forward to giving her husband a very warm welcome when he returned. So she got up, put on her dressing gown, and ordered a bottle of champagne in an ice bucket. As soon as the room service man had departed, she stripped off, put the two glasses beside the bed, and dimmed the lights. It was still well before 11:00 p.m. She closed her eyes and imagined Hugh's return.

Inevitably she fell asleep.

She awoke with a start. The dim light was still on. The clock radio on Hugh's side of the bed showed 2:18 a.m. There was no sign of Hugh. Her heart started to pound. Where was he? Had he gone off with one of the bar girls for the night? No, he wouldn't do that. What should she do?

She dialled Andy's number to check whether he had returned. There was no answer, which was worrying. So she threw on some clothes and hurried down to reception. She told the desk clerk on duty that her husband had said he would return before midnight, but he had still not come back. Nor had his friend. She was very concerned. The clerk asked her where he had gone. When she mentioned Nana Plaza, it was immediately apparent what was going through the clerk's mind. It showed on his face. 'No worry. I think he come back very soon.'

'It's not what you think. He has gone there on business with Mr Andy McInnis. He should have come back before midnight.'

'You no worry. He come back soon.'

The night clerk's English was fairly limited, and it was clear that she was not getting through to him. Very likely, her story seemed implausible.

'I am very worried about his safety. Please ring the police.'

The clerk tried to dissuade her, but eventually and very reluctantly, he acquiesced. He talked for a couple of minutes with someone at the police station. They were speaking in Thai, but it seemed to Ruth that the police were of the same view as the clerk, so she demanded to speak directly with the officer. When she did, she received the same advice in broken English: go back to bed—he'll come back soon.

She tried to explain that he and his friend had gone there on business and that Hugh had promised to be back by midnight, but to no avail. Communication was a real problem. But Ruth persisted, becoming hysterical and raising her voice. Eventually, the Thai policeman told her to go back to bed. He and his colleagues would make enquiries and ring her tomorrow. So in tears, she took the lift and returned to the lonely hotel room.

She put the champagne in the minibar and changed into her nightie. It seemed impossible to sleep. Her mind raced and she imagined all sorts of horrible scenarios. The hours passed. But eventually she cried herself to sleep.

It was a deep sleep uninterrupted by dreams. When she awoke around nine o'clock, daylight was streaming through her window and she felt refreshed. Then the dreadful memory of the previous night struck her like a heavy blow and she felt weak and helpless. She called the hotel operator to ask whether there had been any telephone calls for her during the night. There had been none. She kept asking herself, 'Why did I let him go?'

She did not feel like going down to breakfast, so she ordered some with room service. Although she did not feel very much like eating, she forced herself to eat everything she had ordered in the belief it would give her strength for the day ahead. She then placed the breakfast tray outside in the corridor, took a long shower, and washed her hair. She tried ringing Andy's room again, but only got the voicemail system. Even after the long refreshing shower, her face looked very drawn, or at least she thought so. So she took a longer than usual with her make-up.

It was going on for 11:00 a.m. by the time she felt ready to leave the room. She took the lift down to the lobby and approached the reception desk, which was now manned by an attractive young woman. When she told the receptionist about her husband and Andy and the fact that they had not returned, the immediate reaction of the woman resembled that of the night clerk. In fact it seemed almost a replay of her meeting with the night clerk. Fortunately, the receptionist had far greater fluency in English and began to take a greater interest when Ruth recounted her discussion with the police officer a few hours earlier. When she asked the young woman to telephone the police to ask whether there had been any progress in their enquiries, the receptionist was rather reticent to do so, but relented when Ruth burst into tears and kept pleading with her, and other guests began to look in their direction.

The young woman chatted for a short time with someone at the police station and then communicated what she had learned to Ruth. The female officer knew nothing about the early morning telephone call and could find no record of it. She had checked the formal records for the night and found nothing. The policewoman told the receptionist to tell Ruth not to worry. 'Many husbands disappear for the night in Bangkok and then return in the morning.'

Ruth knew Hugh better, and the fact that both men had disappeared convinced her that something serious had happened to them. She asked the receptionist to demand some action from the police and let her know as soon as possible anything they discovered. The receptionist conveyed this in Thai in terms that Ruth guessed from her body language were more forceful. Ruth thanked her and returned to her room to wait.

Another couple of hours passed and she had another room service meal delivered, but still there was no response from the police. They did not seem interested. What should she do? What should she do? Then she had a thought. 'The embassy—the Australian embassy. Why didn't I think of this earlier?'

She rushed to the hotel guest information folder and scanned the telephone section. There was no mention of foreign embassies. She then worked through the folder more slowly and thoroughly. In a different section, she found lists of temples and churches of different denominations and foreign legations. And the Australian embassy was listed! She picked up the telephone and dialled the listed number. To her dismay, all she heard was a recorded message in Thai and in English. This was hardly surprising, given that it was Saturday. The message, however, did provide an emergency number for Australian citizens. Unfortunately she was not prepared with anything to write down the number. So she hung up, found a pencil and hotel notepaper, and re-rang the embassy number. She now had the emergency number.

When she dialled the number, a woman answered. Ruth said that her husband had disappeared and she needed embassy help. The woman at the other end responded, 'Just a moment. I'll get my husband.'

It was a relief to speak with someone who spoke the same English as she did, and the assistant first secretary listened intently. Ruth explained that they were in Bangkok with a Scot named Andy McInnis who was searching for a man named George Williams, the owner of a bar called Barbies. Her husband and Andy McInnis had gone to the bar early on Friday evening, promising to be back before midnight. Neither had returned and she was very concerned about their safety. Andy McInnis was a private investigator and they had reason to believe that George Williams was a violent man and possibly a murderer. For language and other reasons, she had not really been able to get her message through to the police.

At least Assistant First Secretary Bill Wyndham was taking her seriously. 'I'll speak with my superior and call you back in a few minutes.' He noted the hotel name and telephone number as well as her room number.

It was fifteen minutes before her telephone rang. For the first time, she felt less helpless. Bill Wyndham would come over to the hotel in about an hour, and most likely they would then go down to the central police station together. This was progress. Maybe the police would take some action this time. Did Bill Wyndham speak Thai? She prayed that the answer would be yes on both counts.

It was nearly an hour and a half before Bill Wyndham arrived. He apologised for being late. Since speaking with her, he had had another emergency call for assistance, and then, as usual, the Bangkok traffic had been dreadful. Because of parking problems, be proposed that they take a taxi and leave his car at the hotel.

There were several people in a queue when they entered the main police station, and it was a quarter of an hour before they were able to speak to an officer. Bill Wyndham presented his embassy credentials and immediately received the policewoman's full attention. He spoke in Thai, and observing the conversation, Ruth gained the impression he was reasonably fluent. After about five minutes, he turned to her and explained the conversation. The officer acknowledged that Ruth had telephoned earlier in the day, but there was no record of the earlier 3:00 a.m. call. The police had been very busy and the female officer had no

JOHN POLLARD

further information. Bill Wyndham had demanded that she call the police stations nearer to Nana Plaza and enquire whether they could provide any light on the whereabouts of Hugh and Andy. The officer had suggested that they take a seat for about fifteen minutes whilst she made these enquiries. She disappeared to a rear office and they waited.

About ten minutes later when the officer returned and beckoned them over. Bill Wyndham spoke with her for a few minutes and then turned to Ruth. 'I have good news. Your husband and Mr McInnis are safe. They were arrested at Barbies Bar. They are in a cell at the police station pending formal charges. The bad news is that the owner of the bar claims that they were attempting to extort money from him.'

'That's ridiculous—but at least they're safe.'

'We now have to decide what to do. I suggest that we try to visit them today to get some idea of their side of the story. We may or may not be allowed to speak with them, but we can try. They police may only agree to allow a lawyer to speak with them, in which case we have a problem as it is now Saturday afternoon and we may only be able to get such professional help on Monday. However, we can face that hurdle after we have visited the local police station.'

'Let's go immediately!'

With the traffic, it took half an hour to reach their destination. The building was rather less impressive than the main station they had just come from and rather untidy if not dirty. They entered and were greeted somewhat indifferently by an officer behind the counter. Bill Wyndham greeted the man in Thai and presented his embassy credentials. The man immediately became more attentive, but at the same time seemed rather edgy. Even before Ruth's companion made a request to visit the two arrested men, it was clear that the officer knew why they had come and felt uncomfortable.

Bill Wyndham asked to speak with Hugh and Andy. The police officer hesitated, and then refused the request. In Thai, Bill then responded, 'Mr Webster is an Australian citizen. I have a responsibility for him. Mr Andy McInnis is a British citizen and I shall report his situation to my colleagues in the British embassy. I believe it would be to everyone's interest for you to allow us to speak with your prisoners. In the meantime, I shall be arranging a Bangkok lawyer to take on their case. Here is my card.'

He told Ruth what he had said and asked her to accompany him out of the station. Once outside, he told her that the police officer would doubtless report their interview to his superiors and that there was a good chance that they would be allowed to visit her husband sooner rather than later. Back at the hotel, they agreed to contact each other, day or night, if there was any development. Bill Wyndham then collected his car to drive home, and Ruth returned to her room, still anxious, but feeling rather better now that she knew the whereabouts of her husband and had a strong ally in her battle to gain his release. Rather than eat in her room again, she decided to dine downstairs in the hotel restaurant.

That night, she tossed and turned less than the night before and eventually dropped off into a more relaxed sleep. She slept in and, after breakfast in her room, decided to take a swim in the hotel pool. She called the hotel operator and asked to be contacted immediately if any telephone call came through for her. The swim was refreshing, and she decided to have a light lunch beside the pool. Mid afternoon, she returned to her room and called the hotel operator to confirm that she was back in her room and to check whether anyone had called. No one had.

She watched the CNN channel for an hour or so, catching up with world news, and was just becoming a little bored when the telephone rang. She rushed over, heart pounding, and was very pleased to hear Bill Wyndham's voice. 'I've got good news. The police phoned a few minutes ago and agreed to let us talk with your husband and Andy McInnis. I have already spoken with my opposite number at the British embassy and he will be meeting us there in about an hour and a half. There is not enough time for me to come and collect you on the way. Can you find your way there in a taxi?'

Ruth could hardly believe the news. 'Yes, of course. Please give me the address.'

The three met outside the police station around 6:00 p.m. Inside, the two embassy men showed their credentials to the police officer at the counter and Ruth showed her passport. They were ushered to an interview room, into which Hugh and Andy, both in handcuffs, entered a few minutes later. Ruth was restrained from hugging Hugh. The prisoners were then seated on the opposite side of the large table, facing their guests. An armed policeman sat in the corner.

Hugh and Andy were unshaven and looked dishevelled. They indicated that their joint cell was not very pleasant and they were relieved to see Ruth and her diplomatic companions. They then recounted all that had happened on the Friday night and their discovery that George Williams appeared to no longer be the proprietor of Barbies Bar. They reported that the man now claiming to be the proprietor, a Mr Robinson, had told them that George Williams had sold out with the intention of migrating to Australia. With the policeman present, they could only hint that there seemed to be some sort of relationship between the bar owner and some of the local police. The hints were not lost on the two diplomats.

Bill Wyndham was just beginning to tell the prisoners that he would organise a local lawyer for them in the morning when a more senior police officer entered the room and indicated that the interview was over. Outside, they discussed what they had learned and made plans for the morning. Both diplomats tried to allay her fears when Ruth expressed concern about the possible cost of a lawyer. 'Let's take this one step at a time. We suspect that the police officers in cahoots with Mr Robinson are probably becoming a little nervous with two foreign embassies knocking at their door. They've already changed their minds and allowed us to speak with the prisoners, albeit briefly. With a little luck and a little more pressure from us, we think they may release both men without charges.'

Ruth thanked them both and, accompanied by Bill Wyndham, returned to her hotel. Before he left for home, he assured her that he would call her as soon as he had any further news, whatever the hour.

That call came at six on Monday morning. Ruth woke with a start. She was delighted to hear Bill Wyndham's voice and the news he brought. 'The police called ten minutes ago and announced that Hugh and Andy are free to go. Their explanation seems to be that Mr Robinson had withdrawn his claim that they were attempting to extort money from him, so no charges had been laid and both men are free to go. I have arranged for an embassy car to collect them from the station and bring them to the hotel. You should see your husband very soon.'

'Thank you, thank you, thank you very much. You have been wonderful. I just can't say how much I appreciate all that you have done and all the time over the weekend you have sacrificed away from your family. Thank you from the bottom of my heart.'

'It's just part of my job, and I am absolutely delighted that things have turned out so well. If it's okay with Hugh, Andy, and yourself, I'd like to have a debriefing session with all of you sometime later today. May I suggest three o'clock at the hotel?'

'Of course,' Ruth replied.

Tears of joy and relief flowed down Ruth's cheeks when Hugh arrived half an hour later. The two men now had their passport and wallets back—minus the cash, quite a large amount in Andy's case. Who had taken it? The men from the bar or the police? They would never find out. After Hugh had shaved and showered, they went downstairs for breakfast with Andy, and the three shared their stories of what had turned out to be a long, stressful, and very unpleasant weekend.

The relief they enjoyed gave them renewed energy to meet with Bill Wyndham that afternoon. The diplomat took detailed notes of all that the two men recounted and also asked for further information about George Williams. Andy mentioned his suspicion that the man might have met with foul play, as he had it on good authority that he was the owner of Barbies Bar only a few weeks earlier and the man who now claimed ownership, Mr Robinson, appeared to be very uncomfortable when Andy used the word 'murder' in connection with his search for George Williams. The assistant first secretary took note.

'I'll check whether there is any record of Mr Williams entering Australia or applying to migrate there, and I'll ask my British colleague to find out whatever he can. What are your plans now?'

'I don't want to stay in Bangkok any longer than necessary,' was Ruth's immediate response. 'Hugh and I have already discussed this. We want to leave Thailand as soon as possible, and we are hoping to get on tomorrow evening's flight to Sydney.'

'What about you, Mr McInnis?'

'I still want to locate George Williams—if he's still around. So I'll stay on in Bangkok, but after the experience of this weekend, I'm going to be very cautious.'

'I suggest that you move to another hotel, keep a very low profile, and keep the British embassy informed about your movements.'

# 16

# Delayed Departure

ANDY SUGGESTED THAT they all have dinner together at a good restaurant he knew not far from the hotel. Bill Wyndham thanked him for the invitation and said he appreciated it very much it, but because he had had very little time at home with his family over the weekend, he should really go home.

It was therefore just the three friends who had dinner together. As Andy predicted, it was a good meal. They were all rather exhausted and did not linger long once they had eaten. They arranged to say 'au revoir' after breakfast the next morning.

Back in their room, Ruth and Hugh showered and climbed into bed. They lay there in each other's arms for a few minutes in intimate silence before Ruth whispered, 'Darling, I've got a surprise for you!' She disentangled herself from his arms and walked over to the minibar, where she withdrew the champagne bottle and two glasses. She then threw off her nightie and climbed back into bed. 'It's your job to open the bottle!'

The cork made a very welcome loud *pop*. Hugh dimmed the light, poured two glasses of bubbly, took off his shortie pyjamas, and climbed into bed. It was not very long before they had finished the whole bottle. Relaxed and happy, they turned out the light and cuddled more intimately, each gently exploring the other's naked body. Their lovemaking had begun.

It was still quite early when eventually they fell asleep.

Hugh stirred. It was still very dark and the radio clock read 2:47 a.m. He had the feeling that there was someone in the room. Concerned that he might frighten Ruth, he lay there listening and peering in the minimal light emitted by the illuminated face of the clock radio. Yes, someone was there, near the door. He then remembered that he had forgotten to latch the security chain before they went to bed.

'Who's there?' he asked quietly, and Ruth stirred. Suddenly, the lights came on, and in the glare, he made out the figure of a masked man holding a handgun. Ruth shrieked, but immediately stopped when the gunman pointed his weapon directly at her and quietly but menacingly said, 'Quiet.'

There was a moment's silence, and then, waving his gun from one to the other, he said, 'You come with me.'

'What do you want? Money? Take it from the table there.'

'No. You come with me.'

'We need to go to bathroom and get dressed.'

Hugh got out of bed and helped wrap Ruth in a sheet. She then walked to the bathroom whilst he picked up the clothes they wore that evening and took them into the bathroom. As he entered, she whispered in a frightened voice, 'What do we do?'

Orders came from the masked man: 'No speak. No close door. No use telephone.'

They were in the bathroom for only a couple of minutes when the masked man came to the open door. 'You come now. Quick.'

The frightened couple could see the gun and the man's shadow, and they obeyed his instruction. He indicated that they should go out into the hotel corridor. Once outside, he closed the door and pointed to the fire stairs. They obeyed, the intruder following with his weapon still visible. At the bottom of the stairwell, the door to the car park was open, and he marched them to a small commercial van where an accomplice stood. Their kidnappers opened the rear door, revealing Andy trussed up with rope and his mouth taped. They were soon similarly restrained and the van doors closed.

The engine started and they were on their way somewhere. But where? The back of the van was pitch-dark. Hugh could feel both the others' bodies against him and he could hear Ruth sobbing. He kept asking himself, 'Why did we come to Bangkok? Why did I go to that damned bar?'

The engine droned on for what seemed to be hours. Then the van seemed to slow down and change directions a couple of times. One of the kidnappers, no longer wearing a mask, opened the rear door. 'Toilet,' was all he said as he untied Ruth and pointed to some nearby bushes. It was dawn and they were on a dirt track in a jungle somewhere. When Ruth returned, she was tied up again, and the same procedure was followed with Hugh and Andy in turn, except that with the men, the armed kidnapper walked over to the bushes with them. Hugh was expecting to see the face of one of the heavies from the bar, but the face was not familiar.

The journey resumed, and from the sound of the engine and the motion of the van, it was apparent that they were back on a reasonably main road. A little light started to filter into the rear of the van. But apart from each other, they could see nothing.

A couple of hours passed and the van slowed down and stopped. The engine was turned off. Another toilet stop? Then they heard the sound of a small electric motor and running liquid. The van was being refuelled. Hugh wondered whether they should try to make a noise by kicking the side wall of the van. Andy was in the best position and seemed to be trying to do so, but there was clearly something preventing him from attracting attention in this way. Ruth was on the other side, but there was no way he could communicate with her.

The nightmare journey resumed, and once again they gained the impression that they were leaving the main road and crawling along a dirt road. This time all three prisoners were allowed out of the van, the ropes around their wrists were untied, and with the curt order 'No speak', the tapes were removed from their mouths and they were presented with plastic containers containing a small amount of fish and rice. The food was cold, but they ate it. The toilet routine followed, and then re-taped and re-roped, they were bundled back into the van. The frightening journey resumed.

There were three more toilet stops, but no more food. The small amount of light in the rear of the van gradually dimmed, and the unwilling passengers realised that night was approaching. Eventually the van seemed to leave the main road again and travel for quite some distance along some sort of track. The engine was turned off, and the rear door opened. Both captors stood there, armed. There was a tiny new moon. Hugh peered around. They were surrounded by dark jungle. In front of them was a small boat with an outboard motor, moored at the bank of a reasonably large river. They were ordered out of the van, and the eating routine was repeated. The cold food was again fish and rice.

With her lips now untaped and with fresh tears, Ruth sobbed, 'Where are we going?'

'No speak,' was the response of the shorter captor, but the other replied with what Hugh imagined as a laugh: 'You go Mister George.'

Their meal finished, their mouths were again taped, and in turns, they were allowed a toilet visit behind a small clump of trees. With their wrists and feet untied, they were ordered into the boat, which swayed from side to side as they struggled aboard. The two kidnappers then climbed in. There was barely enough room for five persons, and fully laden, the boat was quite low in the water.

The outboard motor fired, and they were on their way downstream following the current. The man driving kept the revs at a low level, presumably to avoid attracting attention. The boat had no lights. The other kidnapper sat behind the captives with his handgun at the ready. It was difficult to judge, but Hugh estimated that they continued downstream for about an hour before they entered a very wide river. There were no lights on the far bank, which seemed to be the direction they were heading. Given the size of this river, Hugh felt certain it had to be the Mekong. If this were true, then they were about to enter Laos. Whereabouts was another question.

Looking around, Hugh could see lights some distance downriver on both sides, but in the immediate vicinity, all was dark. There were no other river craft to be seen. At the slow rate they were travelling, it took almost half an hour to reach the far bank. The kidnapper driving the boat jumped out and tied the boat up to a tree stump. The other ordered the captives out. They seemed to be surrounded by jungle.

As soon as they were on the bank, their hands were tied in front of them and their legs were loosely hobbled. The shorter kidnapper stood guard whilst the other wandered up and down the bank looking for something. He must have found it, as he signalled his accomplice with his flashlight, and the latter prodded his captives to walk towards the man in front.

It was not easy scrambling along the edge of the mighty Mekong River with hands tied and ankles hobbled. Nor was it easy when they were led into the jungle along a very ill-defined track. The taller kidnapper moved further ahead, obviously looking for something. At times he almost disappeared among the trees as the narrow track twisted. All they could see was the light of his flashlight. Where were they heading? What was in store for them? All three were very frightened. Andy hobbled along a few metres in front of Ruth who was sobbing quietly. Hugh was close behind her, followed by the shorter kidnapper, who lit their way with his flashlight and kept his gun at the ready.

Andy, in the lead and almost in the dark, had a difficult time finding where to place his feet. The tall kidnapper in front was by now almost out of sight a hundred and fifty metres ahead. Suddenly, Andy tripped, and with his hands tied and his legs hobbled, he struggled to get back to his feet. The captor in the rear muttered something, which Hugh guessed was a curse. He pushed past Hugh and Ruth and tried to get the rather tall Scot back on his feet. Andy was almost back standing when he suddenly turned his body clockwise violently and imbedded his right elbow into the throat of the captor. The latter fell to the ground and lay motionless. Andy immediately indicated to Hugh and Ruth that they disappear into the forest and keep quiet. They did so with some trepidation, knowing from their 1999 drive through Laos that unexploded ordinance is always a danger. Andy bent down, turned off the flashlight, and managed to remove the gun from the motionless Thai. The man was probably dead, but to make sure, Andy smashed his head in with the weapon and followed Hugh and Ruth into the jungle, but deliberately stayed closer to the track.

They waited, hearts thumping. Ruth's sobbing stopped as she watched and waited. There was silence for a long time. Then, they could see the light from the leading kidnapper's flashlight again. He was on his way back to find his colleague and their captives. It seemed like an eternity. Eventually he came across the body of his accomplice and bent down to examine it. As he stood up and looked around, Andy raised the handgun he had acquired and pressed the trigger. Even with his wrists tied, Andy was a deadly shot. The tall kidnapper dropped to the ground.

Andy gestured that they should remain quietly where they were whilst he crept forward to check that the man was dead. He came back a couple of minutes later and signalled 'all clear'. The three of them still had their hands tied and legs hobbled. With the help of one of the flashlights, Andy managed to find a rock about waist high with a reasonably sharp edge. He started scraping the rope that tied his wrists on the edge of the rock. The rope was not particularly thick or tough, but even so, it took about ten minutes to cut it. By the time the rope snapped, both his hands were bleeding. He was then able to remove the tape from his mouth, untie his legs, and release the others.

As soon as their mouths were untaped, Hugh and the tearful Ruth thanked Andy profusely. Andy replied with a modest understatement, 'Those years in the SAS weren't wasted after all! I had to do something. From the kidnappers' conversations in Thai, I got the impression that Scarface is buried further along this track and that the boss wanted us out of the way—presumably because he thought we knew he had had Scarface murdered. We were about to meet the same fate. I tripped and made a fuss about struggling to get up again, deliberately. We were very lucky that the taller man went so far ahead trying to find the murder and burial area.'

Most of the night was still ahead of them. So they would be able to leave the scene under cover of darkness. Hugh and Andy agreed that they must be on the Lao side of the Mekong. Whether they were upstream from Vientiane or downstream was unclear. Given the largish tributary into which they had embarked in Thailand, the forest around them and the lack of any nearby lights, as well as the fact that the kidnappers had chosen this place for murder, it seemed that they were probably some distance upstream from the capital.

The clothes Andy had thrown on when awakened in his hotel room contained his passport and a considerable amount of baht that he had obtained only the previous afternoon. Hugh and Ruth, on the other hand, had nothing. One possibility was to find a road and then hitch or take a bus to Vientiane. Hugh and Ruth were familiar with the location of the Australian embassy and felt sure that they could find it. Presumably they could get new passports there and then travel by bus across the Friendship Bridge into Thailand and on to Bangkok. The problem was that they were in Laos illegally, and this would take some explaining to the Lao authorities. They could very well end up in gaol. The two dead bodies might give some credence to their unusual story, but there was then the risk that they might be kept indefinitely in Laos on murder charges.

The other possibility would be to take the boat back to Thailand. They had no idea where they had embarked, but that did not matter. All they had to do was cross the river without being seen, find a road, and hitch or take a bus to Bangkok. The only risk was being caught by Lao or Thai authorities. Presumably the safest route was the one by which they had come—if they could find it.

The other issue was the bodies of the two dead kidnappers. From their 1999 drive through Laos en route to London, Hugh and Ruth were aware that there were areas of the country reputably frequented by bandits. In fact in 1999, they had been advised not to drive from Vientiane to Luang Prabang, which they surmised was not too far away. They mentioned this to Andy. The latter wanted to minimize the chance of them being associated with the deaths of the two men. So they took the two guns with them and headed towards the river. When they reached the riverbank, he carefully cleaned both weapons. He told the others he would throw them into the centre of the Mekong where they would be virtually lost forever. It would then appear to anyone coming across the bodies that their killers, whoever they were, possibly bandits, had weapons and still had them on them. Andy also carefully cleaned the two flashlights so that they could continue to use them and the only fingerprints on them would be their own.

They then walked along the bank upstream to where the motor boat was tied up. Andy checked the controls and got Hugh and Ruth to clamber on board. He then released the rope tying the craft to the tree stump, and pushed off. The motor started easily, and they were soon on the way travelling slowly and as quietly as possible across the giant fast-flowing river. In the light of the faint new moon, they could just see the distant bank. Andy's aim was to reach the Thai side of the river in a darkened non-populated area, but sufficiently close to a lit area that they could find a road without too much difficulty.

They were lucky not to encounter any other craft as they crossed the wide international boundary river and about half an hour later reached the Thai bank. The boat was a problem as it might arouse suspicion and suggest that the killers had travelled to Thailand. Their own fingerprints would also be on it in various places. Thorough cleaning would take hours and might still leave evidence. What Andy wanted to do was scuttle the small craft mid river. He could try piloting it well out into the river and swimming back, but scuttling it would be difficult, and he might be washed a long way downstream before the boat sank and then come ashore scantily clad in an inhabited region. Finding Ruth and Hugh again would also be difficult. So he decided on a risky but hopefully successful approach.

He used some rope to tie the outboard motor in a position that would guide it straight ahead. Then under his instructions, Hugh and Ruth scavenged the bank for rocks that might be used to bash a hole in the wooden hull. He selected one with a slightly pointed end. He began striking the hull near the stern. At first he had no success, but he kept trying, and after some time and a lot of patience as well as blistered and bleeding fingers, he managed to make a small crack in the hull, which allowed water in very slowly. He then searched in the gloom for a rather smaller rock to place over the crack. He then kept bashing the smaller stone with a much-heavier larger rock until the smaller rock burst through the hull and water started to flow in quite rapidly. With the weight of the outboard motor, the level of water in stern started to rise reasonably fast. They pushed the craft out a couple of metres and pointed it towards the middle of the Mekong. Andy started the motor and jumped clear, getting completely drenched in the process. The unmanned craft headed towards Laos, drifting slightly downstream in the current. Hopefully it would continue in that direction and sink well before reaching the opposite bank.

Mesmerised, they watched the boat until it disappeared from sight. Had it sunk? They had no way of knowing. They hoped so. Fortunately, it was a warm night as all three of them were wet, particularly Andy.

When the boat had disappeared from sight, Andy suggested that they wander downstream along the bank towards the nearest lights, where they might find a road of some sort. If they hid out until morning somewhere along the road well away from the houses, they could dry off and hopefully hitch a daylight ride with a lorry heading in the Bangkok direction—whatever direction that was.

As they drew closer to the lights, a dog barked briefly, so they climbed the riverbank well clear of the hamlet, still hoping to find a road, which they did after struggling through some trees and across a field. Which direction led to Bangkok? Walking away from the houses seemed safest for hiding and drying out, even if it did not lead to the capital, so they headed half a kilometre in that direction, found some large rocks in a clump of trees, and sat there waiting for dawn. The rocks were far from comfortable and they got up to stretch their legs innumerable times.

Dawn arrived and they were ravenous. Perhaps there would be a roadside food stall in the village, where they could eat and ask about travelling to Bangkok. They were slightly cold and eager therefore to get moving, but because their sudden appearance from nowhere might look even more suspicious if they arrived in the hamlet at the crack of dawn, Andy suggested that it would be better to wait until the sun was well up before setting off along the road. They agreed.

After what seemed an eternity, they set off. To avoid conversations that might lead to awkward questions, Andy indicated that he would only use English and sign language. At all costs, they should avoid the police who might ask for their passports and report their movements.

It took only about ten minutes to reach the hamlet, the lights of which they had seen the previous night. It was still quite early. As they strolled down the main street, they saw only a few of the locals, who seemed a little surprised at their appearance but otherwise paid them little attention. A couple of dogs barked. Towards the end of the village, an older woman watched them curiously. Andy approached her and in English asked, 'Restaurant?' and mimed eating. She responded in Thai and pointed down the road in the direction they were heading. Andy smiled and thanked her politely in English. They continued walking. Andy revealed that whilst pointing, she had said in Thai that there was a roadside stall selling hot food at the next village, which was larger than hers and not far away.

About two kilometres on, they did in fact come across a larger village and found a woman setting up her stall. They approached her, and this time, Hugh asked for 'something to eat' and mimed what they wanted. She pointed to some stools nearby and asked them to wait.

The woman came over and showed them some meat and rice. Ruth guessed it was pork and quizzed the woman by making 'oink, oink' sounds. The woman grinned and nodded. She boiled the rice over a small gas ring and then cooked the cubes of pork. She served generous portions. Having not eaten, the three travellers ate the basic meal ravenously and washed it down with a fizzy orange drink.

The woman seemed pleased with the strangers' appreciation of her cooking, and after paying, Andy put a question to her as he pointed up and down the road, 'Bangkok?' The woman pointed in the direction they were already heading. She seemed pleased to be able to help. Emboldened, Andrew then took a stick and slowly drew a bus in the earth. She shook her head speaking rapidly at the same time. He then drew a large truck near the bus, pointed to himself and his two companions, and made signs about hitching a ride. At first she hesitated, not comprehending. So Andy repeated the mime. This time she smiled and spoke rapidly, nodding affirmatively. Andy seemed pleased and explained what she had said, 'There is no bus here. You might hitch a ride with a truck to the nearest town with a bus station. It's about ten kilometres.'

They said their farewells with lots of smiles both ways and continued on down the road. After they walked quite some distance, a farm vehicle came along travelling in their direction. They tried to hitch a ride, and the vehicle slowed to a halt. Seeing three people, the driver indicated that he did not have space. They continued walking. Another small truck came by, and the driver accepted Ruth as a passenger in the cabin whilst Andy and Hugh had to travel behind on the rather dirty tray top.

The driver understood that they wanted to take a bus and willingly took them to where they needed to go. Andy thanked him and gave him a generous number of baht. He then started enquiring about buses to Bangkok. 'Bus? Bangkok?' A man standing nearby responded, in Thai interspersed with the occasional English word for the benefit of the foreigners. Hugh and Ruth did not really understand what the man was saying, but Andy, with his Thai, did. There would be a bus to Bangkok in the early afternoon around one, and it would arrive in the capital well after midnight.

They received this information with mixed emotions, elated because they would be back in civilisation that night, where they could shower and put on clean clothes, but depressed because they had to remain tired, dirty, and smelly for so many more hours, even before they climbed on to the bus.

They filled in the first half hour exploring the town and then sat down on a wall to await the arrival of their transport. When it eventually arrived, it was already fairly full. They managed to find three seats close to each other. Ruth was only too conscious of her appearance and felt sorry for the passenger alongside her, who must have wondered what this smelly, dirty, unwashed Western woman was doing travelling by bus to Bangkok.

The man across the aisle from Hugh spoke a little English and, after some initial pleasantries, asked them whether they were tourists and what they had been doing. He was politely curious. Andy, sitting immediately behind, was listening and said 'Hello' to the man. He explained that they were indeed tourists and had been touring some of the nearby Thai country. They had had some car troubles and had had a falling out with their driver, so they had decided to return to Bangkok by bus independently and expected the driver to deliver their luggage to their Bangkok hotel as soon as the car was repaired. Much to their relief, the man seemed to accept the story.

There were relatively few stops along the way, and all of these were sufficiently long to allow passengers to visit the toilet. Eventually around 1:00 a.m., the bus pulled into the Bangkok bus terminal. They looked for a taxi, but without any luck. There were several tuk-tuks nearby. So they hired two of these.

It was close to 2:00 a.m. by the time they reached their hotel, and the night clerk seemed confused and somewhat worried when they asked for keys to their rooms. Part of the problem seemed to be his limited English. He telephoned and woke the manager, who appeared twenty minutes later. The manager spoke good but heavily accented English. The problem seemed to be that the night before their abduction, Hugh

JOHN POLLARD

had informed the hotel that they were checking out the next day so that their account could be finalised. When they did not appear the next day, the hotel staff at first suspected that they had 'done a runner'. They sent someone to the room, who knocked at the door and, when there was no response, entered the room. He was very surprised to find the room in a state of disarray, clothes still hanging in the wardrobe, the safe locked, and money lying on the bedside table. When he informed the manager, the latter telephoned the police, who arrived half an hour later.

The police interviewed the night staff, but no one had noticed anything unusual. The police had requested forensic assistance, and in the meantime, the room was locked as a possible crime scene. The hotel could not, therefore, allow Hugh and Ruth back into the room without police permission. He would now telephone them to inform them of the guests' return.

Andy, on the other hand, had not arranged to check out, and nothing had seemed abnormal when the maid made up the room. She had obviously not noticed the damaged door chain, so he was allowed his key.

Hugh started to plead with the man. 'We have had a very bad experience and are very tired. We haven't slept for the best part of two days. We urgently need to have a shower and go to bed. We are happy to speak with the police in the morning. Please let us into our room.'

The manager indicated that he could not permit them access, and his answer brought hysterical cries and tears from Ruth. 'Please', she sobbed, 'Please let us go to our room and sleep. I can't take any more of this.'

Andy interrupted, 'Perhaps you can let my friends have another room for tonight and inform the police in the morning. We all need a rest, and we won't be very helpful to them if we are too tired and exhausted to answer their questions properly.'

The manager could see that Ruth was close to breaking point, and all three guests looked completely exhausted. What Andy had said made some sense, and it also appealed to him. He could also go back to bed himself and someone else could worry about the problem in the morning. He told the clerk to find an alternative room.

The manager disappeared, and the clerk produced the key for another room. The three exhausted guests headed to the lift area. They reached Andy's floor first, and he asked them to come to his room briefly, where they would discuss what they needed to do in the morning.

The discussion turned out really to be instructions from Andy as to what they should say to the police in the morning. The important thing was that, if at all possible, they should not reveal the deaths of the two men. Otherwise they might spend a very long time indeed in Thailand or possibly Laos while the complicated story was unravelled. They might even spend time in gaol in either or both countries as murder suspects. They had to tell the truth and reveal only sufficient information so as to make their story plausible. They should say that they were kidnapped in the middle of the night by two masked men who took them away from the hotel in a small van. The men had driven them a long way from Bangkok. They believed both men were Thai, but did not recognise either man. The men had given them food and allowed them toilet stops in the jungle well away from the road. At one place, they had managed to escape under cover of darkness and had eventually returned to Bangkok by hitching a ride in a farm vehicle and taking a bus. If they were asked why the men had kidnapped them, they should say, truthfully, that they did not know. If asked whether there were suggestions that the men would be demanding ransom, they should again truthfully say that they had no idea. It was all true, but of course they left out some very important details.

'I see what you're saying, but I'm wondering whether the police will buy our story. The weakest part is explaining how we escaped. Also, we've already been involved with the police in connection with our American friend, Mr Robinson, so aren't they likely to start questioning him? What will happen if the police decide we are holding back information?'

'Okay then. What do you suggest?'

'We/you killed both those men to prevent us from being murdered. We should tell the full story. If the police investigate the Lao part of our story or get their Lao colleagues to make investigations, they should, hopefully, find the body of Scarface, which would make our story hold water and implicate Mr Robinson in both the murder of Scarface and our abduction. I think we should phone Bill Wyndham immediately, tell him the full story, and ask him to be here in the morning when the police arrive.'

'Okay. Maybe you're right. Let's do that. All I want is to avoid any time in a Thai, or worse still, Lao prison. Those couple of nights in the police cell here were more than enough, I'm sure you'll agree! Thailand still has capital punishment for murder, and I'm not sure about Laos, although I suspect it does. I wouldn't want us to be charged with murder and wrongly convicted.'

Contacting Bill Wyndham, however, was not easy. His telephone number was in Hugh and Ruth's original room, currently a crime scene secured by the police. So the only way they could contact him was to ring the Australian embassy again and get the emergency number, and then call that number. When they telephoned the emergency number, they woke someone else they did not know—Bill Wyndham was not on call. They explained their previous involvement with Bill Wyndham and the woman agreed to telephone him immediately and ask him to call Hugh.

It was well past 3:00 a.m. by the time the diplomat called. Hugh gave a reasonably detailed account of their abduction and escape, including the killing of the two kidnappers on the Lao side of the Mekong. He also mentioned that Andy had heard the men, speaking in Thai, refer to the killing of George Williams and his burial near where they managed to escape. Bill Wyndham listened carefully before responding. 'No one has informed the embassy of your disappearance, but then it was only discovered thirty hours ago and the police are only about to start their investigations. Given what you have told me, I think I should call my opposite number at the British embassy and the two of us should come over to the hotel in the morning at say 9:00 a.m. If the police come earlier and take you to the station, we'll come on down there. Why don't you go down to breakfast at around eight thirty and we'll find you in the restaurant? In the meantime, try to get some sleep.'

All three were hungry and they were tempted to order some food from room service. But exhaustion was the greater force. So the two Australians left to find their new room a couple of floors up from Andy. Their hot showers seemed luxurious and so too did their bed. But after the terror of the previous days and the concerns they held about the next few days, it took some time to fall asleep, but when they did, it was a very deep sleep uninterrupted by dreams.

They were awakened by the telephone. It was Andy. 'I'm downstairs in the restaurant. It's 8:45 a.m. and our diplomatic friends are due here soon. The police have not yet arrived. Perhaps the manager has not yet called them.'

Their minds jumped into action. Then, as Hugh was about to put down the receiver, Ruth shouted across the room, 'We've got nothing to wear, only those filthy, smelly clothes.' Fortunately, Andy was still on the line. So Hugh explained the problem and told him they would order a quick room service breakfast and work out what to do. Hopefully the police would allow them access to their old room, at least to gather some fresh clothes.

# 17

# Police Interview

HUGH AND RUTH put on the dressing gowns provided in their temporary room and ordered an urgent substantial breakfast. As soon as it arrived, they ate ravenously. They had barely started, however, when the telephone rang. Hugh picked up the receiver. It was Andy again. 'No sign of the police, but Bill Wyndham and his British counterpart Nigel Llewellyn-Jones have arrived.'

'We can't come downstairs. Why don't you suggest that they come up here with you. In the circumstances, I don't think it's unreasonable.'

A few minutes later, Andy arrived, accompanied by the diplomats. After a few pleasantries and social chit-chat, Bill Wyndham suggested that they go through the whole story. This time, Andy told the story in full detail, with an occasional additional comment from Hugh or Ruth. Since the British diplomat Nigel Llewellyn-Jones had not been intimately involved from the very beginning, Andy explained the reason they had come to Bangkok and described what had occurred earlier at Barbies Bar and subsequently.

When Andy had finished, the diplomat asked, 'The two kidnappers weren't the same ones you encountered at Barbies Bar? You're certain?'

'Definitely. I saw the faces of the heavies at the bar clearly, and I also saw the faces of our abductors clearly. I was initially surprised that the latter allowed us to see their faces, but when I learned from their conversations in Thai that they intended killing us, it was clear that they were not concerned that we saw their faces. My guess is that they were hitmen hired by Mr Robinson and they had previously done work for him. I would guess also that he would not want to use people directly involved at the bar in case they gave him away. I'm sure the police will interview him, and when they do, he and all his henchmen will have perfect alibis. If our abductors were hitmen, they probably have police records of some sort, and we probably could recognise them if the police showed us their 'rogues gallery'.'

Bill Wyndham was the next to speak. 'We certainly have a problem. There are two bodies lying up north somewhere on the other side of the Mekong in Laos. They are presumably those of Thai citizens, killed there by a British citizen with Australian accomplices. The British citizen and one of the Australians were earlier accused by the American owner of a Bangkok bar of an extortion attempt, although he later withdrew this claim. So what do we do?'

He then answered his own question. 'We have to wait and see what the police do. They may feel that they've done their duty when they've made sure the three foreigners are safe. If they take this line, they will ask a minimum of questions and the case will be closed. Andy, Hugh, and Ruth should answer simply and truthfully whatever they ask. Given that the foreigners claim they were kidnapped, however, I think the police will want to identify the two thugs and arrest them. If this line is taken, the police may present Andy and friends with mugshots to look at. If they manage to identify the kidnappers, the police will then go looking for them. Of course, we know they won't find them and why. Indeed, if the suspects turn out to be untraceable, the police will begin to wonder why and start to ask the three of you rather more searching questions about your escape and exactly where and how it occurred. They may even doubt the whole kidnap story.

'Of course the escape details may well emerge in early questioning. As soon as the police realise that both kidnappers are dead and their bodies are lying somewhere in Laos, they have a much more difficult case on their hands. At this stage, they will probably either arrest all three of you or at least impound your passports until the case is cleared up. At this point, you will need a good local lawyer.

'For your defence, it will be important to establish whether there is a body buried at the location where you escaped. This should be relatively straightforward if there is one there and the Lao authorities cooperate. Then, if there is a body there, we will need to establish the identity of the deceased. It will probably be reasonably straightforward to determine whether the body is that of a Caucasian, but full identification is likely to be extremely difficult, even impossible. Incidentally, I meant to tell you earlier that I checked with our immigration department. There is no record of George Williams entering Australia or applying to migrate there.

'Determining who the killers were will be more difficult. With a little bit of luck, it might be possible to establish whether a gun was used and whether it was the same gun used to kill the Thai kidnapper, but that's a long shot—pardon the pun! It's a pity you threw those handguns into the river—we need to tie those unknown killers to Mr Robinson and the bar. That will be very difficult to do so unless Mr Robinson cracks under pressure or he acquired the bar from George Williams illegally or criminally. All told, it won't be easy.'

He turned to his British counterpart. 'What do you suggest?'

'I believe the police will take a serious interest in the case from the very beginning, particularly after the earlier accusations of extortion made by Mr Robinson. The kidnapping claim may sound fishy, and the police may well wonder whether Mr McInnis and Mr and Mrs Webster faked their kidnapping to put pressure on Mr Robinson. We will have to make sure that the Lao police cooperate and examine the area of interest carefully to confirm that there is a Caucasian body buried in that vicinity—as we suspect. We need to inform the Australian embassy in Vientiane about the case and our hope that the Bangkok police will contact their Lao counterparts. We handle British/Lao matters here in Bangkok. Locally, we need to engage a criminal lawyer to represent our three citizens and talk on their behalf with the police. I have someone in mind with an excellent legal record who speaks fluent English. He has helped us on a couple of occasions.'

'What do our three friends say?'

Hugh responded almost immediately, 'What you both say makes a lot of sense. What sort of legal costs would be involved?'

Andy was less enthusiastic. 'What has been suggested sounds sensible. But I'm very worried about the possibility of being extradited to Laos. That's why I took so much care to cover our tracks. The evidence here at the hotel suggests very clearly that we were kidnapped. If the local police accept that we were taken against our will to the other side of the Mekong and I had to kill those two thugs to save Hugh, Ruth, and myself, and they can persuade the Lao authorities that this is the case, then all may go well. Otherwise we're in serious trouble. Hopefully both kidnappers have form, in which case the police should be more sympathetic to our case. Who knows, they might even thank me for doing them a favour! As far as our legal costs are concerned, I am sure Mrs Blum will pay these.'

'Well, what will you do?' asked Llewellyn-Jones.

JOHN POLLARD

'I guess we have to do what has been proposed and bring everything honestly out into the open. I would hope that with two embassies behind us here in Bangkok and the Australian delegation in Vientiane, our chances of being charged with murder or being detained for a prolonged period will be minimised.'

'You can count on maximum assistance from the British embassy, and I'm sure the same is true for the Australian embassy. Since the police have not yet made their presence felt, I suggest Wyndham and I return to our embassies. Subject to your approval, I'll contact the lawyer I mentioned and ask him to make himself available should you need him. Who knows, you mightn't even need him!'

They gave their approval for Llewellyn-Jones to approach the lawyer. As the diplomats were about to leave, Ruth and Hugh raised the matter of their lack of clothing due to their original hotel room being locked off as a crime scene. The Australian diplomat told them that they should ask the police when they came for access to their clothes. If this was refused, they should contact him and give details of their sizes, and he would arrange for someone from the embassy to buy them suitable clothing.

After the departure of the embassy men, the hotel prisoners discussed the conference for a while. Whilst Andy could move freely, Hugh and Ruth found it very frustrating being forced to remain in their room. There was no indication as to when the police would arrive and whether they would allow them back into their original room in the foreseeable future. Andy knew his way around town and offered to go out and buy some clothing for them. They knew nothing about his taste in clothes, particularly female attire, but felt desperate enough to try him out.

When he left, they turned the television on and watched the CNN channel disinterestedly. Half an hour elapsed. Suddenly the telephone rang. It was a call from reception. There were two police officers who wished to speak with them. Hugh explained that because they were denied access to their original room, they had no clothes to wear and were dressed only in the dressing gowns provided by the hotel. They suggested that the police come to their room. There was a murmur of conversation at the other end and then the reception clerk came back on line. 'The police will come up to your room.'

Hugh and Ruth waited, hearts pounding. When the inevitable knock at the door came a few minutes later, the strain on their faces was showing as Hugh opened the door. The senior officer introduced himself in very good English and then introduced his colleague.

Hugh's initial reaction was that a rather senior man had been sent to interview them, possibly because of the earlier extortion claim issue and the involvement of the British and Australian embassies at that time. The officer tried to put them at their ease. The problem was that the room was not designed for interviews. It was small and there were only two chairs. As they stood uncomfortably, Hugh explained why they could not come downstairs and told the police that their friend Mr McInnis had gone out to buy them clothes. The officer did not know that Andy had also been kidnapped (or claimed to have been kidnapped), and he therefore wanted to speak with him also.

The policeman was very courteous and suggested that they meet later in the day. 'I am sorry that you could not go back to your room last night. I shall arrange for our forensic team to examine your room thoroughly today. You will be allowed back later this afternoon. We will want to speak with Mr McInnis also. So I will come back at 4:00 p.m. I hope this is okay with you. You may leave the hotel, but please be back at that time. I will ask the hotel to make a small conference room available.'

The man was very courteous and seemed to be trying hard to be friendly. Hugh and Ruth both felt more relaxed and smiled as they shook hands with the departing officers.

It was lunchtime by the time Andy returned with clothes for his friends. They were quite pleased with his choice. At least they could now leave their room! Half an hour later, they met up downstairs to go out to lunch at a nearby restaurant. Andy, of course, was anxious to learn as much as possible about the earlier police visit. Hugh and Ruth gave a brief account of the short interview and told Andy that they thought that the senior police officer was professional and friendly, which boded well for the follow-up interview.

The same two officers arrived punctually at 4:00 p.m. and called the Australians to the small conference room. This time they sat down at a small table and the senior officer placed a notebook in front of him. He started in a formal fashion with the question, 'Why are you here in Bangkok?'

A simple answer would be to say 'As tourists'. It would be true, but it would inevitably lead to closer probing, and the police officer would suspect that they were being less than cooperative. So Hugh provided a more detailed response.

'We are here as tourists with our expenses paid by a client of Mr McInnis. She wanted to reward us for having been helpful in discovering

JOHN POLLARD

the fate of her son who disappeared mysteriously in India in 1968. Mr McInnis is a private investigator.'

'How were you able to help?'

'We were travelling in Afghanistan, Pakistan, and India in 1968, and it just happened that we met the young man very briefly in Pakistan and India.'

'What happened to this young man?'

'He travelled for a time in a friend's car. He was somewhat of a mystery and disappeared suddenly from our party.'

'Our party?'

'Not a party in the social sense. Perhaps I should have used a different English word. What I meant was our group. There were four of us travelling in two cars. He invited himself to travel with us under somewhat mysterious circumstances and hid in the car—a van—most of the time. Our friends thought he was scared of something or someone.'

'So what happened to him?'

'No one knew until a few weeks ago, when we returned to the Indian Himalaya with Mr McInnis. We guided him through the region where we last saw the young man. Mr McInnis made numerous enquiries of men who might have seen the missing man, and very much by luck came across a man who, not only had seen the killer, but had also been forced to help bury the young man's body. Even thirty-five years later, the Indian man was still terrified of the killer. DNA testing revealed that the body was indeed that of the woman's missing son.'

'How was he murdered?'

'Shot.'

'Did you find out who the killer was?'

'Almost certainly—yes. As I said a moment ago, an Indian in the Himalaya identified a man in a photograph shown to him by Mr McInnis as the man who forced him to help bury the body. This does not prove that the man in the photograph actually murdered the young man, but makes it most likely.'

'Who is the man in the photo?'

'George Williams, who used to own Barbies Bar.'

'How did Mr McInnis obtain the photo of Mr Williams and know his name?'

'Mr McInnis did tell us, but it was somewhat complicated, and I have forgotten. It goes back to the initial search for the missing young man in

1969. You will have to ask Mr McInnis for the details—unless my wife can answer your question.'

'No, I've forgotten the details too.'

The officer, who had written down a lot of short notes during the interrogation, wrote down rather more at this stage. The two Australian waited, wondering what was coming next.

'Why were you, sir, and Mr McInnis in Barbies Bar the night of the police raid?'

'Surely that is obvious. Mr McInnis was hoping to meet Mr George Williams, the owner of the bar. Mr McInnis made enquiries about him at the bar on two successive evenings, but received no help from the men behind the bar or the young women he spoke with.'

'Why were you in the back room with Mr Robinson when the police arrived?'

'Two men we believed to be armed demanded that we go out the back. We expected to meet Mr Williams, but instead, we met Mr Robinson.'

'Why did Mr Robinson claim that you were attempting to extort money from him?'

'I don't know. Perhaps he was trying to get us discredited or locked up, or at least out of the way.'

'Why would he want to do that?'

'I don't know. Perhaps he had something to hide. He certainly seemed very worried when Andy—Mr McInnis—said that we were looking for Mr George Williams and mentioned murder. Just before the police raid, he told us that George Williams had sold him the business and had migrated to Australia.'

'Why did Mr Robinson drop his allegation of extortion?'

'Again, I don't know. You would have to ask him. The British and Australian embassies had become involved. Perhaps he feared that his claim would be discovered to be false and that during the extortion investigation he would be asked some awkward questions. But I simply don't know.'

'Let me now ask you about your disappearance from this hotel three nights ago. Please tell me in detail what happened.'

Hugh did not like the use of the word 'disappearance' rather than 'abduction' of 'kidnapping', but he tried to continue his account of events without showing any irritation. 'It was the night after my release from police custody. We ate an early dinner with Mr McInnis and then returned to our room where we drank a bottle of champagne before bed. We turned out the light and fell asleep.'

He was about to continue when the policeman interrupted, 'But you had sex—yes?'

Ruth jumped up from her seat and screamed at him. 'You filthy, dirty man. Our intimate lives are none of your business. My husband and I have been happily married for forty years. Why do you interrogate us like criminals when you should be out finding those responsible for our abduction? Leave us alone, you pervert.'

She tried to storm out of the room, only to be stopped by the other policeman.

Hugh was furious. 'Let my wife go, or are we under arrest? We have been cooperative trying to assist you fully with your enquiries. Because of your irrelevant, distasteful question and your implication that we staged our abduction, we refuse to answer any further questions.'

The senior officer realised that he had gone too far. 'No, you are not under arrest and you are free to go. I apologise for what I have said which has offended you. You must realise that I have to find out everything relating to this matter, and I was just trying to indicate to you that I already know quite a lot even before you tell me the details. You may go if that is your wish. You are also free to return to your old room. I will need to continue with the questions later, however, even if I have to get a court order to enforce it.'

'If this happens, we will answer your questions, but only with a lawyer present, representing us.'

With that, they both got up from the table and headed towards the door. The senior officer signalled to his offsider to let them pass. There were no smiles or handshakes as they marched out the door.

Back in their room, Hugh called Bill Wyndham. He reported that initially the interview had passed pleasantly until the officer asked a question in a manner that seemed to imply that they might not have been kidnapped at all and soon after asked an irrelevant question about their private life that had nothing to do with the case. After that, they refused to answer any further questions. They were allowed to leave the small conference room where the interview had taken place. They had not had a chance to speak with Andy.

The police summoned Andy to the conference room more or less immediately after Hugh and Ruth had left. He recalled that the Australians had reported a quite friendly initial encounter that morning with the police. The reception he received, however, was civil—almost cold—and in no way friendly. He wondered what had transpired a few minutes earlier with his Australian friends.

Although he did not know it, his interrogation started with virtually the same questions as had been directed at his Australian friends. There were, however, additional questions about his experience and activities as a private investigator. They also spent a lot of time questioning him about the American who had disappeared thirty-five years previously, the reason the case had been reopened, and how Mr and Mrs Webster had become involved. The senior officer took notes throughout the questioning.

Questions about the abduction started. 'Tell me about how you were kidnapped.'

Andy explained that he had been fast asleep in the early hours of Tuesday morning when he was awakened by two masked armed men breaking into his room. 'They switched the lights on as they burst in. I was still in bed and couldn't do anything. In broken English, the taller man told me to put on some clothes and come with them. They then marched me along the corridor and down the fire stairs to the car park in the basement, where my mouth was taped and I was tied up. Then they shoved me into the rear of a small white van. There were no windows.'

The senior officer wrote a few lines and they made a remark in Thai to his offsider. It was clear from these remarks that the police did not really believe their kidnapping story. He decided immediately that his answers to the remaining questions in this interview would be very brief and provide only the least information possible. He would certainly not reveal that he spoke and understood Thai.

'The hotel room keys are electronic and all the rooms have chain latches on them. How did the men burst into your room?'

'As you and I both know, the modern electronic keys in hotels are not very secure and are easily copied. Mr. Robinson could well have done this. He had our keys while we were in police custody. I didn't hear the men opening the door. The first sound I heard was the sound of a bolt-cutter snapping through the chain. If you look at the door to my room, you will see that the chain has been cut. Didn't your men discover that? It's still broken.'

It was clear from the officer's face that he was angered by Andy's questioning of the police work, but he continued his interrogation without commenting.

JOHN POLLARD

Later, when Andy reported that the kidnappers had stopped using their masks after they were well clear of Bangkok, the interrogating officer asked, 'If I showed you photographs of the men, could you identify them?'

'Aye,' was Andy's immediate answer.

The officer muttered something to his colleague, which Andy did not catch.

When the questions led to the boat journey across the Mekong into Laos, the officer did not have to say anything to his offsider about not believing the story—his face told it all, as did his questions.

'So you were taken to the jungle on the Lao side of the Mekong by these two armed men. Why do you think you were taken there?'

'To be murdered.'

'Why would these men kidnap you with the intention of killing you? Wouldn't they want you alive so that they could demand a ransom?'

Andy could have told them at this stage that he was fluent in Thai and had heard them say that they were going to kill the three of them, but he chose not to reveal this information. Instead he responded, 'Because we were investigating a murder and we were looking for George Williams. I believe that George Williams has been murdered and that Mr Robinson is implicated. For that reason, he wanted us out of the way.'

'Why would these men you say you could identify want to take you all the way to a remote part of Laos to kill you?'

'I don't know. My guess is that it is a good place to hide bodies. They obviously knew the area well, even in the dark, and I believe that Mr George Williams's body is there too. They did say to us while we were still in Thailand that they were taking us to "Mr George".'

'How is it that you managed to escape and are now back in Bangkok?'

'When we were walking in the jungle away from the Mekong, one of the men walked some distance ahead, apparently looking for the place where we would be killed. He was in a hurry and got a long way ahead. I managed to surprise the man still with us and disarm him. When the other man found that we were not following, he came back searching. I surprised him and managed to disarm him as well. I then had both weapons. We returned to the boat and came back to Thailand and left the two kidnappers in Laos. In the morning, we hitched a ride on a farm truck and then took a bus back to Bangkok.'

'How is it that you were so successful in overpowering these men?'

'Before I became a private investigator, I was in the British military and undertook special advanced training.'

'Where are the guns?'

'At the bottom of the Mekong.'

This brought an unbelieving smile from the officer, almost a laugh. 'Why would you do that?'

'If we encountered Lao or Thai officials, I didn't want to be caught carrying illegal weapons. It was bad enough that my friends did not have their passports with them. I had no further need for the guns. So I threw them overboard in the middle of the Mekong.'

Another disbelieving smile showed on the police officer's face.

'Where did your escape take place?'

'In a jungle on the Lao side of the Mekong. I knew that it was the Mekong, simply because of its size. I didn't know where on the Mekong until I got back to Bangkok. The bus we took stopped at a town called Loei. When I got back to my hotel room, I looked for the town in my Thai Atlas and found that the Loei River joins the Mekong a bit further north. There is a road bridge over the river just before it joins the Mekong. I am almost certain, therefore, that it was on the Loei River that we were forced on to the boat and that the location of the spot where we were to be murdered was more or less directly opposite the Loei River mouth.'

The police officer looked thoughtful. 'That's all for the moment. I will need to interview you and the Australians again.'

Instead of returning to his room, Andy went straight to Hugh and Ruth's room and knocked at the door. Two very cautious voices called out 'Who's there?' and peered through the peephole. 'Andy.' They undid the chain and let him in.

# 18

# Wasting Police Time

THE THREE FRIENDS spent some time comparing notes. One thing they agreed on was that the interviewing police officer did not believe that they had been kidnapped, or at the very least, had serious doubts about their story. What would convince him that they were telling the truth? Should they simply leave Thailand, never to return, and forget the whole thing? Would the police allow them to leave? Although their passports had not been impounded, there seemed a good chance that they might. They suspected that the police were watching their movements and may well have instructed the hotel to report them if they checked out. Andy still wanted to find George Williams, dead (as he now believed) or alive. Should they tell the police immediately that there were two dead bodies lying in the jungle on the other side of the Mekong? What would the police do then?

Their immediate concern, however, was their safety. Presumably the police, if they had not already done so, would be interviewing Mr Robinson and he would then know that Andy, Hugh, and Ruth were back in Bangkok. Would there be another attempt on their lives? Or would the boss believe that such an attempt would be too risky and might very well convince the police that their kidnapping claim was true, increasing police suspicion of his involvement in that kidnapping?

They could try hiding. The risk then was that the police might believe that the three foreigners were up to tricks again. If they hid but revealed their location to the police, there was the risk that their whereabouts might be passed on to Mr Robinson by one of the local policemen whom they suspected of corruption.

After a lot of discussion, they decided to call Assistant First Secretary Bill Wyndham again and ask for legal assistance. Andy would telephone his local private investigator contact and seek his assistance in ensuring their safety. In the meantime, Hugh and Ruth would keep themselves securely locked in their room.

When Hugh called the embassy, the Australian diplomat revealed that he had already spoken with his British colleague, who would contact the lawyer he had previously recommended and ask him to meet the abductees at their hotel the next morning at nine. That was good news.

Andy telephoned half an hour later. His Thai contact had suggested that they keep their present hotel rooms and leave most of their belongings there, but move temporarily to a hotel where he (the Thai contact) had good relations with the management. Andy and the Australians would have adjoining rooms and the contact would arrange a guard outside. Hugh and Ruth were more than happy to accept this arrangement. To minimize the possibility of anyone noticing that they were moving out, they were advised to take as little as possible with them and make it look as though they were just going out for a while.

They decided to meet for dinner downstairs early that evening and move hotels afterwards. In the meantime, there was little to do except watch the CNN television channel. Before they met, however, they were summoned to the front desk. There was a police officer to see them. They soon discovered why he was there. He showed them a short document all in Thai and demanded 'passport'. Andy immediately asked the clerk on duty to translate the document. She did, and it was quite clear that a court or equivalent had authorised the police to impound their passports, and they reluctantly handed them over.

After dinner, they took a taxi to the centre of the city, where they were met by the local private investigator and the man who would guard them overnight. The latter then drove them to their new hotel. It was not particularly luxurious, but it was clean and provided all that they needed. Before retiring, they had a drink at a small empty bar upstairs. With the police likely to be looking for them and thugs hired by Mr Robinson possibly doing the same, they wondered how long they could hide out in their new 'home'. The plan was for their guard to collect them each afternoon or evening at varying times from different locations within a short tuk-tuk distance from their original hotel, with a similar arrangement for their return to their original hotel each morning. The guard would use different cars from time to time. Sometimes they would take a taxi rather than a tuk-tuk. To conceal their nightly absences, they were instructed to make their beds look slept in and use the shower and bathroom in the original hotel.

With the heavy Bangkok traffic, it was necessary to set off quite early the next morning so as to be ready to meet the lawyer retained on their behalf by the British legation. Mr Suramongkol turned out to be a very pleasant man, around 50 years of age. He was accustomed to Westerners having some difficulty with his name. 'Please, simply call me "Sura".' His clients reciprocated with their first names. Sura handed each of them his card, in Thai on one side and English on the reverse.

After a few minutes of pleasantries, they got down to business. Sura's English was very good indeed. 'I lived in England for five years.' It was clear too that he had memorised all the details of their case as recounted by Bill Wyndham. Andy filled him in with the most recent developments, including the name of their new hotel. Hugh and Ruth felt reassured when he indicated that he approved their new security arrangements.

Ruth was by far the most visibly worried of the three clients. 'What do we need to do now?'

'I suggest that we wait to see what action the police take. In the meantime, with your permission, I will go down the central police station and report that I am your legal representative. I will present my card and tell the police that I must be present when they interview you. To this end, I have prepared letters for each of you to sign giving me this authority. The letters are in Thai and in English. I shall also ask the police why your passports have been impounded. Do you feel happy with this approach?'

All three replied in the affirmative.

Hugh's thoughts were racing forward to being interviewed again. 'Andy has told the police that he overpowered the kidnappers one after the other. What should we say in an interview if the police want greater detail?'

'That will depend on the circumstances at the time. I will be there to advise you and protect your position. Who knows, with the British and Australian embassies behind you and with—I hope I don't appear immodest—a leading legal representative, the police may decide to give you back your passports and allow you to leave Thailand. Of course, from your perspective and particularly that of Andy, this may be less than satisfactory, as it would leave too many loose threads. I know you are very worried, but let's wait and see what action the police take.'

'Okay. Thanks.'

Sura told them that he had the name and telephone number of their other hotel, but to protect their security, he would not use that information except in an emergency. In all other circumstances, he would meet them at their original hotel and leave messages for them there. 'I'll go down to the police station now and then report back to you here by phone. If you're not available, I'll leave a message to call me back. I always have my cell phone turned on.'

Despite the cloud still hanging over them and the fact that they were now more or less prisoners, the meeting gave them a rather more positive view of the future and their increased confidence showed on their faces. There was nothing to stop them leaving their hotel, but they thought it wise to remain there, at least until lunchtime, in the hope that they received a call from Sura.

He telephoned just before lunch and Hugh took the call. The officer who had already interviewed them was noncommittal about the intentions of the police and gave no indication that he was impressed by the interest being shown by the British and Australian embassies. From Sura's clients' point of view, the fact that the police wanted to interview them again that afternoon was more alarming. Sura could sense their anxiety even over the telephone. 'Don't worry. I'll be there all the time, and I'll give advice and intervene as appropriate. Detective Charoenkul wanted to arrange the interviews in the hotel's small conference room today at 4:00 p.m. I insisted that I needed time to talk with my clients and he agreed to start the interviews at 5:00 p.m. If you're agreeable, I'll meet you in Andy's room at 4:00 p.m. to agree on our strategy. In the meantime, go and have a good lunch!'

They followed his suggestion and returned to the fish restaurant by the river where they had dined in rather more relaxed circumstances not so many days earlier. They tried to unwind a little, but in the circumstances, this was difficult. Andy wanted to return to his room at 3:00 p.m. to bring his colleagues at head office up to date on developments. He wondered whether the police were now eavesdropping on his e-mail, but thought this unlikely and believed that the security was good. He would risk it, but send the e-mail from an Internet café rather than the hotel. He suggested that Ruth and Hugh stroll around for a while before going back for the preliminary meeting with Sura. Ruth, however, was feeling very insecure. So the three returned together.

Sura spent most of their preliminary meeting trying to make sure his clients remained calm during the following interviews. 'You must remain calm and not react angrily to any of the questions, even if they seem ridiculous or insulting. If I think a question is inappropriate, I will definitely intervene and say so. If I think you should not answer a question, I will advise you so. You must answer all questions truthfully, but don't give any more information than you need to.'

'What do we say if we are asked details about Andy overpowering the two thugs?' asked Hugh, and all three looked intently at their lawyer.

'That's a very tricky matter. If you reveal that Andy killed both of them, the police will have no evidence of this unless they seek the assistance of the Lao authorities and ask them to search the area. The Lao police should find the bodies quickly after a bit of a search. What we must ensure is that they also search the nearby area very thoroughly in the hope that they discover the remains of George Williams. If the Thai police don't ask their Lao counterparts to do this, then we must ask the Australian legation here in Bangkok to ask their Vientiane colleagues to put some pressure on the Lao police to search more thoroughly.

'I think that ultimately we will have to go down this path, but that we should not try to get there too quickly. Andy has already told the police that he could identify the kidnappers if shown their photos. Hopefully, before we get to the details of their deaths, I will have the opportunity to demand mugshots of any likely local undesirables so that Andy can look through them and, if we're in luck, identify either or both of the offenders. Of course, there's still the chance that their faces won't be among those we are shown. If Andy does identify one or both of the men, the police may still not believe your claim to have been kidnapped. They might even think that Andy simply selected one or two men from the photos.'

The lawyer turned to Hugh and Ruth. 'The police will probably expect you to be able to corroborate Mr McInnis's mugshot choices. Do you think you would be able to recognise them in photos?'

'Maybe' and 'I think so' were the two responses.

'Then I think we should try to move the process in this direction. I will remind Detective Charoenkul that Andy has already told him that he would be able to recognise the two men if shown their photographs. I will then try to force the police to produce as many mugshots as possible of likely candidates. This will mean that the formal interviews will have to be deferred and take place at the police station. I will try to have Andy questioned first, alone. Hopefully, he can identify the criminals. I will then have them show the mugshots to Hugh and Ruth, either together or separately, and hopefully you will corroborate Andy's evidence. If you are unsure about a photo—and some of them may be rather poor photos—you should say "I think this one" or "It may be either this one or possibly this one". The important thing is that you hit on one that is the same as one selected by Andy. If you don't see anyone you recognise, you must, of course, say so.'

The telephone rang suddenly. It was the front desk, announcing the arrival of the police. They wanted Andy in the now-familiar small conference room.

When Andy and his lawyer entered the room, it was clear that they were in for a frosty reception. The detective was clearly not happy that a leading lawyer had been retained to represent the foreigner.

'I have spoken with Mr Robinson, and he told me that you were in his bar trying to cause trouble and that he interpreted your presence there as a threat to extort money from him. He withdrew his claim of attempted extortion when he recalled that you had not actually demanded any money from him. He says that your accusation of him paying men to kidnap and murder you is quite ridiculous and that for some unknown reason you are trying to stir up trouble. He did not know why.

'So I need to ask why you are stirring up trouble and wasting valuable police time.'

'I am not.'

Andy's short sharp rebuttal of what Detective Charoenkul implied in his question obviously surprised him. It also clearly annoyed him. There was a pregnant pause while the officer gathered his thoughts. He was about to follow on with another question when Sura interjected.

'It is clear that you do not believe what my client has told you about the kidnapping. I presume you have checked the chain on his hotel room door and found that it has been cut. Surely, this should give some credibility to his story.'

The policeman did not respond, and both Andy and Sura got the impression that the police still had not checked the door and its chain.

'In the previous interview, you asked my client whether he would recognise the kidnappers if he was shown photographs of them. He answered yes. As his legal adviser, I demand that he be given the opportunity to look at police photographs of all possible suspects before you continue accusing him of inventing a kidnapping story and wasting police time.'

The detective was clearly not pleased by the direction the interview was going, and he was now on a back foot. 'Okay. Nine in the morning at the police station.'

'Do you want my other two clients to attend also?'

'Yes.'

The interview was over, and Hugh and Ruth were not summoned.

When their security guard met them at the prearranged location that evening, he presented Andy with a sealed envelope, which contained a brief note from the Bangkok private investigator, which read as follows:

> *I have found some further information about Mr George Williams. As my company told you some time ago, he was the owner of Barbies Bar. According to legal records I have now seen, he sold his Thai business three weeks ago to a Mr James Robinson. You will have observed that the bar in Bangkok is always very busy and presumably very profitable. So the sale price of 15,000 baht seems very low.*
>
> *I also found the address of his apartment and spoke with the building manager. Mr Williams is still listed as the tenant. The next rent payment is due in about three weeks. Occupants of the neighbouring apartments say they used to see him quite regularly, but they have not seen him or anyone else go to his apartment recently.*

Andy read the note to the others and commented, 'Very interesting.'

# 19

# Police Mugshots

THEY SPENT ANOTHER night without incident at their alternative hotel and were driven to a location near their original hotel early the next morning. After walking back to the hotel, they returned to their rooms to shower and change. A short taxi ride then brought them to police headquarters for the next interview. Andy was taken to one room, and Hugh and Ruth to another.

Detective Charoenkul produced a folder containing what seemed to be about fifty shots of rather unpleasant-looking men and instructed Andy to look through them and identify the kidnappers. The private investigator thought it a very small folder for a large lively city and surmised that the detective may be testing to see whether he would simply select two faces from the folder at random. He worked through the photographs slowly and meticulously. It took about ten minutes, and as he closed the last page, he shook his head. 'Not there.'

The detective spoke briefly in Thai to his assistant, who left the room and returned with a rather larger folder, which he placed in front of Andy, who immediately started looking through the photographs. Once again he did this slowly and meticulously. After about fifteen minutes, he stopped. 'That's one of them—the taller one.'

The policeman noted the name of the man. Andy then resumed his sifting through the mugshots. Several minutes later, he stopped and studied the face in front of him intensely. 'I think that may be the other man. I'm not entirely sure. If it is, it's not a very good photo. I'll keep looking.'

Detective Charoenkul noted the name of the man.

It took another ten minutes for Andy to look through the remaining photographs, but he found nothing. When he had finished, his lawyer spoke for the first time. 'My client has identified the two men who kidnapped him and Mr and Mrs Webster. When are you going to accept his story?'

'Your client has selected two faces from our files and claims that they kidnapped him. We will interview both men. I hope for his sake that he is not wasting any more of my time. But first, I want to show the same files to the Australian couple and see whether they tell the same story. You will not be allowed to speak with them until after I show them the files.'

The police, accompanied by Sura, entered the other room occupied by Hugh and Ruth. The Australians looked apprehensive and remained tense when handed the shorter file of photographs. They examined each photograph carefully and paused for quite some time over one.

'Maybe that one?' suggested Ruth.

'No, definitely not. Look at his nose. It's far too straight,' was Hugh's reaction, and Ruth, looking intently at the photograph again, agreed.

They kept looking and found nothing. Detective Charoenkul then produced the larger file, and they worked slowly through it. When they came to the man Andy had identified, Hugh looked at it very carefully. 'I think this might be one of them, although I'm not completely sure. These police photos are not ideal. What do you think?'

'I was about to select that man too. I am pretty sure that it's one of them, but not 100 per cent sure. Let's look through the remaining photos and come back to this one.' They continued looking, but failed to come up with another suspect. They turned back to the photograph that caught their attention earlier and studied it very closely again.

They nodded to each other. 'We're almost sure that's one of them.'

Their lawyer looked at the detective. It was clear from his expression that he was obviously having second thoughts about the kidnapping story. 'May I speak with my clients now?'

'Yes.'

Sura told the Australians that Andy had positively identified the same man and that Andy had also identified another, but with less certainty.

'So do you believe us now?' Ruth shot at the policeman.

'I will bring those men in for questioning,' was the response.

They were allowed to leave and took a taxi back to their official hotel for a post-interview conference. After three days of police scepticism, they were all on a high. But there was now a more serious issue to address. The police did not know that the kidnappers were dead. If they allowed the police to go searching for them and eventually found that Andy, Hugh, and Ruth knew that they were dead, the police would not be pleased, and the accusation of wasting police time would haunt them again.

'Should I make a formal statement to the police?' asked Andy.

'The police will know the usual haunts of these men. If they go looking for them, they will wonder why they can't locate them and will come asking more questions. There is a remote chance that you'll get your passports back before this happens, in which case you may be able to leave Thailand, but I doubt this will happen. The police still believe the kidnappers are alive, and as things stand at the moment, they will want you here in Bangkok to give evidence about the kidnapping.

'But let's assume that you are allowed to leave. The police are sure to discover ultimately that the two men have been killed and you will then be the prime suspects. They will seek your extradition, or the Lao police might do so. Given that Thailand and Laos still have capital punishment, your own government may refuse your extradition, but it's not a good position to find yourselves in.'

'Okay. I'll make a formal statement. You know all the facts and could probably draft it. But would it be better for me to write the initial draft and then allow you to rework it from a Thai legal perspective, yes?'

'I think that would be good and reduce the need for drafts going back and forth between us. Perhaps you can write your draft this afternoon. I can then work on it tonight. If you're happy with what I write, I'll prepare a Thai version as well as the English one. Before I give it to the police, however, I want to be sure they are in fact taking the kidnapping seriously.'

'Okay. I'll draft it this afternoon and phone you.'

## 20

# Interminable Waiting

ANDY SPENT A couple of hours that afternoon preparing his draft statement and Sura worked on it overnight. By the following afternoon, the statement was ready in both English and Thai. The statement made it clear that Andy was fluent in Thai and he therefore understood what the kidnappers were saying to each other, particularly in relation to his and his friends' impending fate.

For Andy, Thai was a spoken language; he had not really learned to read the script. So Sura read the Thai version of his statement to him. He was satisfied with what he heard.

Late that afternoon, Sura rang police headquarters and asked to speak with Detective Charoenkul. He was not in. Much to Sura's surprise, the police officer returned his call an hour later. The detective's opening words gave Sura the immediate impression that he was now taking the kidnappings more seriously. 'I apologise I was not here to speak with you when you phoned. I was actually attempting to find the man identified positively by your clients.'

The conversation continued in their native tongue in a progressively more relaxed fashion.

'Did you make any progress?'

'A little. One of his associates told me that he was with him last week, but had not seen him since then. He said he planned to be away from Bangkok for a few days. I told the man I wanted to speak with him as soon as he returned.'

'And the other man identified with less certainty by my client?'

'I hope to visit his family tomorrow.'

The icy formality of the past two days was starting to thaw.

'Thank you for this information. I shall tell my clients. The reason that I phoned earlier was to ask you about these matters, and you have told me what I wanted to know. I believe that my client Mr McInnis may have further information which did not come out in the earlier interviews and which could be helpful in your enquiries. We could come down to the police station tomorrow morning. If you would like this, how would nine in the morning suit you?'

'I would appreciate any additional information. Yes, 9:00 a.m. would be fine. I can visit the family of the second man after that.'

Andy had mixed feelings when Sura called him a few minutes later. On one hand, the police would now know the whole story and the mysterious disappearance of George Williams might be solved. On the other hand, having killed two Thai citizens across the border in Laos, he could be charged with their murders and possibly face a long jail sentence or worse. But if the case they had made about being kidnapped dragged on without a solution, they could be kept in Thailand for a very long time. On the positive side, it had to be clear that he had acted simply in self-defence and in defence of his companions. He agreed to go with his lawyer to the police station in the morning and told Sura that in the meantime he would update Ruth and Hugh.

Detective Charoenkul was certainly much more friendly when he met with Andy and Sura the next morning. As Sura had intimated, the policeman now seemed to believe their story, or at least their having been kidnapped—and most likely, kidnapped by the men they had identified in the police photograph album.

He accepted Andy's English and Thai formal written statements from Sura and read the Thai version slowly and carefully. When he had finished, he turned to Andy and, speaking Thai, asked him, 'When did you learn to speak Thai?'

Andy responded speaking Thai, 'My ex-wife is Thai. We lived here for a year early in our marriage and I learned to converse in Thai.'

The conversation continued in the local language. 'Why did you not tell me this earlier?'

'It did not seem relevant to my answers to the questions I was asked. It was only when I sat down to prepare the formal statement you have in front of you that it became clear to me that it was very relevant to my understanding of our kidnappers' murder intentions.'

'You have admitted killing two Thai citizens in Laos. This is a very serious admission and changes the course of my investigation. I still hold your passport and those of your friends. You are all to remain in Bangkok while I follow up this new development.'

Sura entered the conversation, still in Thai. 'It is clear from my client's statement that both men were killed by him to prevent him and his Australian companions being murdered. They should not be treated as criminals and should be allowed to return to their homes as soon as possible. What do you intend to do?'

'The evidence in Laos is obviously crucial. Sometimes relations between our police force and the Lao police are difficult. Other times they are straightforward. I will need to contact the Lao police and seek their cooperation. Getting them to search the area should not be too difficult. If there are bodies in the area, the question of jurisdiction arises, and there may be political ramifications too—involving Thailand and Laos, and possibly Australia and the United Kingdom, even the USA. I intend contacting the Lao police today.'

Sura was intent on the police finding all the possible evidence relating to the kidnapping and he pointed out that there were a number of loose threads that needed tidying up. 'The white van must still be up north beside the Loei River. Surely this is an important piece of evidence. It should have the kidnappers' fingerprints on it, and there should be some forensic evidence that my three clients were in the back.

'As you know, my client believes that Mr Robinson is behind the kidnapping. Although my client knew nothing about Mr Williams being murdered, it seems that Mr Robinson thought that he did. Rent on Mr William's apartment is not due for three weeks. No one has seen him there in the last three weeks and the neighbours have seen no one going to the apartment. There may be relevant evidence about Mr William's disappearance there. Mr Wyndham of the Australian embassy has told us that the Australian immigration authorities have no record of Mr Williams entering Australia or applying to migrate there, as Mr Robinson has claimed.'

Detective Charoenkul listened attentively. His response to Sura's remarks revealed that he was now taking the case even more seriously. 'Mr McInnis's written statement makes it clear that the case is rather larger and more complicated than it appeared initially. I intend to get additional support to follow up all these matters.'

In the taxi on their way back to the hotel, Sura suggested to Andy that copies of his formal statement be given to the British and Australian embassies with a request that copies also be forwarded to the Australian

Vientiane legation. 'I was also thinking along these lines,' was his client's response.

Sura waited two days before telephoning the detective. It was a long wait for the three Bangkok detainees. Detective Charoenkul had been true to his word. Local police in the north had found an abandoned white van, and a forensic expert had been dispatched to dust the vehicle for fingerprints and look for other evidence. His report was expected in a couple of days.

The piece of information Sura and Andy were most concerned about—discussions between the police and those north of the Mekong—was also positive. Detective Charoenkul's chief had made contact with the Lao police, who, after consultation with their minister, had agreed to send police stationed in the area to search for the bodies. He had not heard back.

Andy, Hugh, and Ruth felt pleased that their story was now seemed to be accepted by the police. They were still in limbo, however, unable to leave Bangkok and not knowing whether or when they would be allowed to leave. Andy kept his office updated with developments and was gratified, although not surprised, when told that Mrs Blum had agreed to continue paying their living and legal expenses.

Another couple of days passed before Sura telephoned the police for an update on their investigations. Detective Charoenkul was again cooperative and they spoke in Thai. 'I had a phone call from Vientiane only an hour ago. The local police in Laos have found two bodies which we believe are probably those of the kidnappers. The bodies were badly decomposed and had been damaged by birds or animals. As far as the local police could determine, one had been shot. The other appeared to have died from head injuries.'

Sura took a mental note that the policeman now referred to the men as kidnappers. 'Did they mention any other bodies or evidence of graves?'

'No. I reminded the Vientiane police of our suspicion that there may be other bodies nearby. They told me that they are sending two forensic specialists to the site and the local police have been instructed to look for evidence of other bodies but not to disturb anything until the experts arrive. The Lao police are being very cooperative.'

'What about my clients? Do they still have to stay in Bangkok?'

'Yes. They are central to the whole investigation.'

'And Mr Robinson. Are you investigating him?'

'Depending on what the Lao police discover, I may well interrogate him.'

'What about his story of Mr George Williams migrating to Australia? As I told you previously, my information is that no one of that name has entered Australia recently. Is there any record of him leaving Thailand?'

'My first priority is to discover all that has happened across the border in Laos. Checking the possible departure of Mr George Williams from Thailand will be part of my investigation when I get the information from Laos.'

The detective's lack of interest in Mr Robinson was frustrating and Sura could not understand why. On the other hand, there was definite progress in Laos and the officer was now referring to the two men as kidnappers. The reaction of Hugh, Ruth, and Andy was much the same when he recounted his conversation with the policeman.

Three days dragged by. Hugh, Ruth, and Andy were now getting used to the wait. They were now relaxed enough to venture out to a number of not-too-conspicuous restaurants. Inevitably, of course, their conversation always turned to their kidnapping and subsequent developments. Given their prolonged time in Thailand, it was fortunately they all really liked Thai food. They continued to sleep guarded at their alternative hotel.

A telephone call to Sura from Detective Charoenkul brought some very interesting news. The Lao police had discovered three bodies buried in shallow graves a little further into the jungle. Judging by the state of the bodies, the forensic investigators judged that one had died a few weeks ago. The others had been in the ground much longer. All five bodies were being taken to Vientiane for autopsies. The body that had been in the ground for only a few weeks appeared to be Caucasian.

The way the detective reported the information made it clear that he now believed what he had been told from the beginning by Andy and the two Australians. Before Sura had a chance to question him, he volunteered more information. 'I intend interrogating Mr Robinson thoroughly.'

The waiting seemed interminable. Although all the developments Sura was able to report were helpful, there still seemed to be no end to the investigation and their freedom appeared to be as remote as ever. Another week came to an end. The following Monday, Sura telephoned Detective Charoenkul, who reported on his interview with Mr Robinson. The bar owner again denied any involvement in the kidnapping and, when shown photographs of the two kidnappers, denied recognising them. Charoenkul also interviewed the men behind the bar, two of whom admitted that they recognised photographs of Andy and Hugh copied from their passports. 'They were causing trouble with the boss.'

The detective showed them the police photographs of the two kidnappers. Both denied knowing them. 'But the way they reacted when shown the pictures, I suspected that they may be lying. I intend having them brought into the police station for further questioning.'

Sura asked whether there was any information from Vientiane relating to the autopsies.

'I was promised that I would be told the outcome of the autopsies by tomorrow. If I haven't heard by then, I'll phone the police there and request an update. As soon as I know the results, I'll phone you.'

The policeman was being very helpful now, and Sura said 'Thanks' warmly.

It was Wednesday morning when the promised call from Detective Charoenkul came.

'The senior police officer in Vientiane phoned this morning. Autopsies have been performed on all five bodies. The two unburied bodies were of Thai or Lao men. Papers in their clothing indicate that they were from Thailand. One man had been shot. The other had a broken neck and head injuries. The other three men had been shot. One of the buried bodies was Caucasian. He was killed only a few weeks ago. The other two bodies were either Thai or Lao and had been in the ground for at least a year. They had both been shot. A bullet was found in one of them, and it appeared that the weapon used to kill the unburied man was the same as that used to shoot the Caucasian.

'The Lao authorities have promised to send a full written report by the end of the week. In the meantime, they have asked me to keep your clients in Bangkok. I intend doing so.'

# 21

# Murder Charges

W HEN IT ARRIVED, the formal report of the Vientiane police held no surprises for Andy and his friends. But a communiqué from the Lao government two days later brought bad news. The Lao People's Democratic Republic was seeking the extradition of Mr Andrew McInnis and Mr and Mrs Hugh Webster to face murder charges in Laos in relation to the two men Andy had admitted killing and suspicion of the murder of the other three unidentified men. The news made headlines the next day in the Australian press and was also prominently reported in the British and US newspapers. The Thai press also took a great interest in the case, causing the three foreigners to remain closeted in their alternative hotel. They ordered in simple takeaway meals.

Bill Wyndham telephoned Hugh as soon as the news broke and promised the maximum possible consular assistance. Nigel Llewellyn-Jones did the same for Andy. Immediate consultations took place between the Australian embassies in Bangkok and Vientiane with Canberra and the British embassy with London.

Sura continued to pursue the police for updates on their enquiries, and Detective Charoenkul reported further evidence supporting the kidnapping story. The white van was a rental vehicle that had been reported stolen some time back, and the name of the person who had rented it coincided with that of the second man identified from the mugshots but with less certainty by Andy. Fingerprints of both men had been found in the cabin. A small piece of tape was found in the rear of the van that had dry saliva on it.

It was apparent that the Detective Charoenkul was now keen to help the three foreigners, whose story he previously doubted. He asked each of them for saliva samples, and DNA testing showed that the tape had Hugh's saliva on it. Everything added up.

There was no progress with the American bar owner, however, who stuck to his earlier story. Detective Charoenkul decided to bring in for questioning the barman who, when shown mugshots of the kidnappers, had seemed to recognize one of them but then denied it. The man was in police custody for thirty hours on suspicion of collaboration in attempted murder, but on his release, the police had what they needed: a confession that his boss had sent him to find someone to get rid of the American and his friends so that they would cease bothering him. It was now time to bring in Mr Robinson.

When the police went to arrest him, the bar owner had fled. The barmen initially denied knowing where he was. They were taken into custody and, after a day in the police cells, revealed that Mr Robinson had left Bangkok by car travelling south. The police immediately put out a search warrant for him nationwide and he was apprehended trying to drive across the border into Malaysia at Betong. A day later, he was securely locked in a Bangkok police cell, charged with complicity in kidnap and attempted murder. He continued to deny any involvement. When confronted with what the bouncer had told the police, he changed his tune slightly. 'My man must have misunderstood me. His English is not very good. I only wanted them away from Bangkok so that they would no longer harass me.' He was evasive when asked how and why Andy was harassing him.

Sura added an account of this interview and the other recent developments to his detailed written summary of the case. This report would be helpful if he had to defend Andy or all three foreigners in court. In the short term, he advised them to forward copies of his report to their respective embassies and request that their ambassadors make it clear to the foreign ministers of both Thailand and Laos the context of the two killings so that the authorities in both countries clearly understood that self-defence was the sole reason for the two killings.

In Bangkok, the Thai foreign minister met the Australian and British ambassadors. The Australian ambassador gave the minister Sura's report, which was in Thai as well as English. He then explained why he had requested the meeting and summarised the main points in the report, emphasising the fact that the killings had taken place in self-defence and that the full Thai police report would confirm the truth of the lawyer's report. The minister asked a couple of questions and then remarked that if it were a case of self-defence, the Kingdom of Thailand was unlikely to agree to the three being extradited to Laos to face murder charges, but he would have to discuss the matter with his cabinet colleagues and in particular the interior minister, who was responsible for the police.

Up north in Vientiane, the Australian ambassador requested a meeting with the Lao foreign minister. Australia was an important aid donor to Laos and had been such over many years. It had in fact financed the Friendship Bridge across the Mekong that connects Thailand and Laos and over which vehicles change from driving on the left in Thailand to driving on the right in Laos. Amongst the other aid projects provided by Australia was assistance clearing unexploded ordinance left from the Indochina war—a huge problem for the impoverished nation. Although the two countries had markedly different political systems, relations were generally good, and the minister readily agreed to meet the ambassador to discuss the case. The Australian embassy handled consular matters for Britain and the Australian ambassador also argued the case for Andy.

Because of the different languages involved and the complexity of the case, the embassy provided the minister with a copy of the Sura report prior to the meeting and the Lao minister was well informed about all the issues when the ambassador arrived. They discussed all the major points in the case, and the ambassador emphasised the fact that Mr McInnis had no choice but to kill the two kidnappers if he and the two Australians were to escape death. The minister appeared to appreciate the argument put to him and promised to discuss the case with the minister of public security responsible for all police matters.

A week went by. In Australia, friends of Hugh and Ruth were asking questions of their parliamentary representatives and giving solid character references for them. Their children were distraught and had to contend with journalists telephoning at all hours and visiting to ask for information and pose stupid questions as to how they felt. They could not believe that their parents had been accused of murder. In Canberra, questions continued to be asked of the Australian foreign minister, who responded by saying that the Australian government was having discussions with the governments of Thailand and Laos through the usual diplomatic channels and was doing all it could. In Bangkok, Andy, Hugh, and Ruth could no longer bear hiding in their hotel and ventured out a couple of times, running the gauntlet of the press and curious onlookers.

Sura spoke with Detective Charoenkul a few times, and the latter revealed that the interior minister had requested a copy of his report. The lawyer and his clients felt that this would surely help their case, at least as far as the Thai legal system was concerned. There seemed to be some progress at the diplomatic level too. The Thai foreign minister called the two ambassadors to his office, where he told them that the official Thai police report had been sent to the Lao foreign minister and that he had had discussions with his Lao counterpart. He was hopeful that he would have more to report soon. In the meantime, the Scot and the two Australians were free to move about in Bangkok, but the police would continue to hold their passports.

Andy still remembered the reason they had all come to Bangkok and asked Sura to enquire at an appropriate moment as to whether the police had investigated George Williams's apartment, and if so, whether they had found anything of interest. Detective Charoenkul was forthcoming.

'The Lao chief forensic officer faxed me two days ago with photographs of the body of the dead Caucasian. They found nothing on his clothing that immediately identified him. The only item of interest was a key and they faxed me a photo of it. The body was not a pretty sight—the face had been almost completely destroyed by the gunshot, but the key might provide a clue. I sent two of my officers to search Mr George Williams's apartment. It was immediately apparent that the key could not be the key to the apartment. From the state of the place, it appeared that Mr George Williams left suddenly, but intended returning. They found three illegal handguns in a locked cupboard, and these are now in our possession. My officers had to break into the cupboard, but before they did so, they photographed the lock, and as far as we can tell from the faxed photo, the lock appears to be of the same type as the key found on the dead man. They also found his passport.

'The Lao police also sent me photos of the two men your client confessed to killing. It was not possible to identify them from the photos, but their clothing contained personal items revealing their names. The men were the ones identified by your clients.'

All the news seemed positive when Sura reported back to his clients.

# 22

# Political Impasse

ALL HUGH AND Ruth wanted to do was to go home. They had lost all interest in staying on in Thailand as tourists. Over the first few days of their detention, before the murder charges had been laid and the Lao government had requested their extradition, they had done a little more sightseeing in Bangkok. Now, all they did was laze around the hotel pool, swimming occasionally and reading. Andy wanted to get back to the US as soon as possible too, but to complete his mission, he needed to find out for certain the fate of George Williams and come to a definite conclusion about the connection between Williams and the death of Dan Blum. The police investigations and international political negotiations seemed interminable. As far as the Australian ambassador could tell, the Thai authorities now seemed to accept the account given by Andy and his Australian friends and were prepared to accept that the killings took place in self-defence. Their lawyer Sura had gained the same impression from his discussions with the police detective.

The sticking point seemed to be that the Lao minister of public security suspected that Mr McInnis had shot the Caucasian man a few weeks earlier with the support of the two Thais. Then, anxious that the men might reveal what he had done, he had taken them at gunpoint to the lonely jungle location in Laos and killed them. One of the men had died from the same gun as that which killed the Caucasian man. To cover his tracks, he had then thrown the weapon into the centre of the fast-flowing Mekong, or claimed to have done so. The Lao minister of public security also could not rule out Andy having been involved in the killing of the other two unidentified Thai/Lao men buried nearby.

The Australian ambassador in Vientiane met with the Lao foreign minister several times. The meetings were amicable, but the minister of public security was intransient and the foreign minister could do nothing. It was a political impasse.

Andy held a green card, which enabled him to work in the USA. The authorities there would have a computer record of his movements in and out of the country. He therefore requested the British ambassador through First Secretary Llewellyn-Jones to approach his American counterpart for a certified copy of his movements into and out of the USA over the previous year. The information came through duly stamped and certified a week later. It was clear from this statement that Andy could not have been in Thailand or Laos at the time the post-mortem investigation indicated the murdered Caucasian man had died.

The police still held Andy's passport, so this was not immediately available to corroborate the information. But what they now had was sufficient for the British ambassador to call on the Thai foreign minister and seek to clear up any further doubt the Thai authorities might have about Andy's involvement in the death of the Caucasian. The meeting was very productive, and the foreign minister promised to examine Andy's passport and then have direct discussions with the Lao foreign minister.

The Lao minister of public security eventually rather reluctantly accepted that according to the information provided by the US authorities, Andy could not have killed the Caucasian, but that did not rule out his having been involved in the killing of the two unidentified men. Because the date of their murders was far from clear and Andy had actually visited Thailand briefly eighteen months previously, it was possible that Andy was their killer. The minister also pointed out that the two Australians had been driving in Thailand and Laos three years earlier en route to London. So he could not rule them out as suspects. What he did not have, however, was a motive. A political impasse had been reached.

Andy tried to keep his mind on the Dan Blum case and forget their current difficulties.

It was possible that one of the weapons discovered in the locked cupboard in George Williams's apartment by Detective Charoenkul's men was the same as that used to kill the young American. The investigation company in Mumbai had the bullet found in Dan's spine. If he asked Detective Charoenkul for assistance and the detective agreed to help, there was a risk that the policeman might try to go through official channels and involve yet another government. It could be years then before anything was resolved, and it might also lead to awkward questions from the Indian police, resulting in serious complications for the Mumbai forensic team.

Andy was also hesitant to ask that the bullet be mailed to him from India. If the parcel went astray, a crucial piece of evidence in the case would be missing. The Indians had told him that the calibre of the bullet was about 6.4 mm (a quarter of an inch). If none of George Williams's weapons was of this calibre, it would be pointless requesting further details from Mumbai. On the other hand, if one of the weapons was of the right calibre, it would be worthwhile asking for blown-up photographs of the bullet in the hope that the markings revealed could be matched with the Williams weapon. He decided to speak with Charoenkul, who of recent weeks was far more approachable.

When he telephoned, the detective was unavailable. Andy left his name and said he would try again later. He deliberately chose to telephone from their original hotel. He was somewhat surprised, therefore, when Charoenkul later returned his call at their hideaway hotel. Clearly the police had tracked them down, and the worrying point was who else knew their night location. With the bar owner Robinson in custody and under suspicion in connection with their kidnapping, the risk of further violence seemed unlikely. He decided not to tell Hugh and Ruth in case they worried, and he made no comment to Charoenkul.

'Hello, Mr McInnis. How are you? Our friends in Vientiane seem to be delaying things, don't you think?'

'Aye. Thanks for returning my call. I'm fine, but I wish I could go home.'

The detective ignored Andy's latter remark. 'You phoned. There must have been a reason.'

'As you now know, everything that has happened here is a consequence of a murder that took place in India thirty-five years ago. I am wondering whether one of the weapons found locked in George Williams's apartment might be the gun which was used in the Indian murder. I phoned to ask whether you would be kind enough to give me the details of the weapons found by your men in his apartment.'

There was silence at the other end of the telephone.

'Hello. Are you still there, Detective Charoenkul?'

'Yes. I'm still here. I was just considering what you said. I don't think there is any reason why I shouldn't give you this information if it will help. Perhaps you might come down to the police station tomorrow morning at nine thirty and I'll give you a list. I might even show you the guns!'

'Thanks very much. I really appreciate this. I'll see you in the morning—and thanks so much for phoning.'

Andy could hardly believe how easy it had been. Detective Charoenkul had certainly changed his attitude towards him and his Australian friends!

The next morning at the police station, he was given a list of George Williams's weapons—all handguns: a Steyr TMP semi-automatic, a Beretta 950 Jetfire semi-automatic, and a Glock 10 mm automatic. With his special military experience, Andy immediately recognised all the weapons. The Steyr and Glock were of Austrian origin, and Berettas came originally from Italy. Detective Charoenkul called a junior officer, who reappeared a few minutes later with the three Williams weapons sealed in plastic bags. He proudly showed Andy the pistols, which the latter examined closely. The ex SAS soldier knew that the two Austrian weapons were of more recent origin and could not have been used in the Indian killing. Berettas, on the other hand, had been around for almost sixty years.

'Is any of the weapons of interest to you?' Charoenkul asked.

'Possibly the Beretta. The other two are too modern. I'll have to get further information from Mumbai.'

Andy was becoming even more certain that the Thai detective wanted to help.

'If I get details about the bullet found in the spine of the murdered man and clear photos of the bullet showing any markings, would you be willing to get your forensic department to compare the characteristics of the Beretta with the Indian murder bullet?'

'Yes. I believe I can justify it as being relevant to the matters here in Thailand.'

Andy thanked the policeman warmly and promised to call him as soon as he received the information from Mumbai.

Back at their official hotel, he prepared a handwritten fax to send to the Mumbai forensic expert.

*Dear Mr Bandopadhyay,*

*I have been shown a weapon in Bangkok which might be the one used in the Rampur murder. I would very much like to be able to confirm whether or not it is.*

*Would you please be kind enough to send me as much information as you can about the bullet discovered in the body? It would be very helpful if you would take a number of photos of the bullet from different angles and enlarge these so that a comparison can be made by the Bangkok police with a bullet fired from the weapon found here.*

*It would be best if you do not send the detailed information by fax. Instead, would you please send it by courier or certified mail to me at the address at the top of this page, enclosing the photos? Please do not send the bullet in case it goes astray.*

*Thanks very much.*

*Andy McInnis*

He deliberately did not mention the type of weapon found in George Williams's apartment in case it influenced the answer he received back from India.

Much to his surprise, Andy received a telephone call two days later from Mumbai. He was told that the bullet was somewhat oxidised on the outside but was almost certainly from a .25 ACP cartridge. The team in Mumbai had cleaned the slug a little and there were some discernible markings that would have come from the pistol rifling. They had photographed the slug carefully from several different angles, and these photographs and some enlargements were already on their way to Bangkok by courier. The ballistics adviser had indicated on the enlarged photographs some of the markings that could be relevant.

Andy was a little surprised that the Mumbai investigator made no reference to the request the Lao government had made for his extradition to face murder charges. He must surely have known. The Scot put it down to formal Indian politeness. He thanked him for telephoning and told him that he was looking forward to receiving the couriered documents.

What he had been told was exciting news. The Williams's pistol used a .25 ACP cartridge, and Andy was not aware of any other pistols using the same ammunition, although there probably were some. He telephoned Detective Charoenkul, told him what he had learned, and promised to call him when the couriered documents arrived.

He did not have to wait long. The documents arrived two days later, and this time Detective Charoenkul came to the hotel to meet Andy and collect them. He told the Scot that according to the information the police held, there was a very limited range of pistols using .25 ACP cartridges. Most were older pre-Second World War models. George

Williams's Beretta pistol was first produced in 1952. The only other comparable model according to their records was a German Walther from the 1960s, although there could be others. Andy gave the detective the documents and asked that they be returned when his forensic team had finished with them.

# 23

# UK Enquiries

ANDY'S HEART POUNDED when the hotel reception put through a call from Detective Charoenkul two nights later. 'I have good news for you, Mr McInnis. Our ballistics experts have examined the Beretta found in Mr Williams's apartment. They believe that this pistol is probably the weapon used to murder the young man in India. They emphasised, however, that they could not be a hundred per cent sure.'

The change in the policeman's behaviour towards Andy from what it had been at the start of the investigation into their kidnapping weeks earlier could not have been more marked. His manner now was almost that of a friend. Obviously he was also becoming interested in the wider case. Andy decided therefore to ask a couple more questions related to the investigation.

'Thank you very much indeed. Have you positively identified the murdered Caucasian man?'

'There is strong evidence that it is Mr Williams, but it's not conclusive. We sent our top forensic man to Vientiane last week with the lock from the cupboard we broke open at Mr Williams's apartment and it matched the key found in the dead man's pocket. The Lao police also agreed to our forensic investigator taking DNA samples from the body, which he later analysed here in our laboratory. I sent these and other details about Mr Williams to London to see whether the British police could help with the identification. Unfortunately they had nothing on their files relating to Mr George Williams. They told us that the passport he used was false, so very likely George Williams was not his true name. They promised to try to help if we found his true identity. Even then, getting a DNA match for him would still be a remote chance.'

'I believe I can help. George Williams's real name is Patrick O'Connell and he has a serious criminal record in England dating from the 1950s, including imprisonment for manslaughter. He was born in Liverpool. They won't have any DNA information from those times, but they might be able to track down a relative and obtain that person's DNA.'

'Thank you, Mr McInnis. I will e-mail London today.'

The Scot could hardly believe that some of the threads of his investigation were finally being tied together, and he put another question to the detective.

'Have there been any developments with Mr Robinson?'

'We have interviewed him many times and put him under some pressure, but he always maintains that he had nothing to do with your kidnapping or the murders of any of the men discovered in Laos— probably because he fears the possible penalty he could receive. With the information given to us by his two men and some circumstantial evidence, we are convinced that he sought hitmen to rid himself of you and the Australians, but he still denies being involved. Proving this will be more difficult. We intend charging him with soliciting killers to murder you and Mr Williams. Whether the evidence we have so far will be sufficient to convict him is uncertain, but we intend to try. His two men continue to emphasise that they had nothing to do with these matters. They also provided other information, naming two local police who regularly received payments from their boss and previously from Mr Williams. Those two police have been suspended from duty and will be facing corruption charges. Mr Robinson will also be charged with corruption.'

'Do you think these developments will help us in our fight against extradition to Laos?'

'I intend writing an updated report. I will be suggesting to my superiors that they recommend to our minister that your passports be returned and you be allowed to leave Thailand. Of course our government may not accept the recommendation, but I would hope that it does. If it does, and the Lao government is provided with all the updated information, it may possibly drop its extradition request, although it is not easy to predict how it will react. I note that in the international news today, the Australian foreign minister will be making an official visit to Thailand next week as one of several visits to South-East Asian capitals, and Vientiane is included on the itinerary after Bangkok. If we move fast, it may be possible to provide the Australian embassy with information that the Australian foreign minister could use in discussions with the Lao foreign minister.'

It had been quite a long conversation. As soon as he had hung up, Andy telephoned Hugh and Ruth's room. They were not there. He found them a little later in the hotel restaurant. They were naturally delighted with the news, causing Ruth to exclaim, 'I can almost forgive him for his behaviour during our first interview.' She had forgotten that Andy did not know the more private details and was relieved when he did not enquire.

The English police had a file on Patrick O'Connell and they responded quickly to Detective Charoenkul by e-mail.

*We have several men named Patrick O'Connell in our files. The one which meets your description was born in Liverpool in 1934. He had several encounters with the law as a juvenile. In 1955, he was involved in a failed armed robbery when he killed a bank teller. He was convicted for manslaughter and received a 7-year gaol sentence. There was considerable community disquiet at the leniency of the sentence, and the bank teller's family took it very badly. He was released after six years. Since then we have nothing on him in our files.*

*The scar you reported is very clear in one of the attached photographs taken at the time of his conviction in 1956, aged 22.*

*There is no record that he ever held a British passport. The one you quoted him as possessing in your earlier enquiry under the name George Williams was clearly false. Presumably an earlier version of this passport enabled him to leave the UK in the early 1960s and travel elsewhere.*

*As far as DNA testing is concerned, we will have to search for a close relative. It is doubtful whether O'Connell's parents are still alive. He had a younger half-brother, Wayne Roberts (different fathers), whom we might be able to trace, but it could take time. If we do locate him, there is no guarantee that he will cooperate and provide a sample. We'll do our best.*

*Robert King*
*Detective Inspector*

# 24

# Self-Defence

TRUE TO HIS word, Detective Charoenkul immediately prepared an updated report that was quickly passed on up through the police chain of command and on to the minister. The detective clearly stated that the police were satisfied that Andy had acted purely in self-defence and that, with the signed statements of Mr McInnis and Mr Suramongkol and other information, they had sufficient evidence to prosecute Mr Robinson without recourse to court appearances by the three foreigners. The minister accepted the police recommendations that the three passports be returned, and Andy and his friends be allowed to leave Thailand. The foreign minister immediately informed his Lao, Australian, and British counterparts of his government's decision and sent each a copy of the full police report.

Ruth and Hugh could hardly believe it when two police officers arrived at their hotel with their passports, informing them that they were completely free and could leave Thailand whenever they wished. They rushed back to their room to telephone home with the good news and told their family that they hoped to get a flight back to Sydney the next day. Their children were ecstatic.

Andy also planned to fly out the next day. There was little point remaining in Thailand to await possible news from the English police, who might take weeks or longer to track down George Williams's half-brother. Andy knew beyond reasonable doubt who had killed Dan Blum and that the killer himself was now dead. The Thai police were certainly keen to confirm the Caucasian's true identity, and if their DNA investigation proved that it was that of Patrick O'Connell alias George Williams, he would have finished solving the mystery for Mrs Blum.

The three freed friends and Assistant First Secretary Bill Wyndham enjoyed a lavish celebratory meal that night. On learning who they were and aware of their recent good news, the restaurant manager generously provided a complimentary bottle of champagne. They were all on a high when they returned to their original hotel and enjoyed yet another drink at the bar. They were free—free from any fear of criminal charges in Thailand—and going home. The Lao extradition request still hung over their heads, but it was unlikely their own governments would hand them over to the Lao authorities, given the information the Thai government had provided and the Lao capital punishment possibility.

Compared with the publicity their case attracted when the Lao extradition request was announced, with the possibility that they might be executed if convicted, the press reports over the next few days in their home countries were almost invisible. As Hugh remarked later to family and friends when they were safely back home, 'Good news doesn't sell papers!'

There were tears of joy and relief at Sydney Kingsford-Smith International Airport when the couple were met by their children, and the excitement and emotional relief continued to flow in the car as their son drove them home. The following Sunday, most of their extended family gathered for a barbeque lunch to celebrate their safe return and hear their account of all that had happened.

Andy had no one to meet him at the airport, but his colleagues gave him a hero's welcome as soon as he entered the office the next day.

They had been back at their respective homes more a week by the time the Lao government responded to the decision of the Thai government. It informed the three other governments directly involved that it was rescinding its extradition request and issued a brief statement to the international press, which again showed relatively little interest.

*The Government of the Lao People's Democratic Republic has withdrawn its extradition request for the two Australians and the British national involved in the killing in Laos of two Thai men. Detailed police investigations have revealed that the three foreigners, Mr and Mrs Webster and Mr McInnis, were kidnapped by the Thais who intended murdering them. The Government is satisfied that the three persons acted only in self-defence.*

For Andy, Ruth, and Hugh, the long nightmare was over.

## 25

# Epilogue

ON HIS RETURN to America, Andy informed Mrs Blum where the investigation stood. He told her about the half-brother of her son's killer and what the English police were trying to do and promised to contact her the moment he received any further information.

Three months went by and then, almost unexpectedly, a report arrived on Andy's desk from Detective Charoenkul. The English police had managed to track down George Williams's half-brother, a retired bus driver, who had had no contact with his older brother since the latter's imprisonment. Locating the half-brother had been a tedious and painstaking process. When asked to provide a DNA sample, the man refused to cooperate. 'He ceased to be my brother when he killed that man and went to gaol. He hasn't contacted me and I haven't tried to contact him. I was very pleased when he disappeared out of my life.'

Then, a week later, and for reasons known only to himself, the retired bus driver changed his mind and agreed to provide a saliva sample. Perhaps he was simply curious—he did not give a reason. DNA testing revealed that, with a high degree of certainty, George Williams was indeed his half-brother.

As soon as he received the news, Andy telephoned Mrs Blum. He told her the results and explained that they simply provided definite confirmation that the Caucasian body uncovered in Laos was indeed that of her son's killer, George Williams. The killer of her son was dead, killed by a Thai hitman. His client was not surprised by the news and simply remarked, 'Those who live by the sword die by the sword.'

She continued, 'I realise the case is now closed, but I would like to meet with you to discuss some of the issues which arise from it. You know of course that I am no longer young and it is difficult for me to travel far from home. Would you be kind enough therefore to come here?'

They made an appointment to meet two days later.

Andy had kept her informed of developments at every stage of the investigation, but even so, given the emotions she must be feeling, he was not really looking forward to the meeting. He hoped she would not ask for details that he believed would be very painful to her and difficult for him to discuss. He was also conscious of the fact that they had not discovered the reason Dan was killed, and he feared that this question might arise in their discussions. His personal view was the same as that surmised by Tom Childs decades earlier—that it must have been drug-related, but this was simply a hunch, there was no hard evidence, and he knew from the earlier investigation records that Mrs Blum would not accept this explanation. To some extent, it was no longer relevant. He hoped she accepted this.

He was pleasantly surprised how warmly she welcomed him and how composed she looked. She clearly realised that the case was closed and did not ask any of the awkward questions he feared. Instead, she raised the matter of where Dan was buried. She told him that her elder son, Ben, a hero, killed in action in Vietnam, was buried in the Arlington cemetery.

'Is Dan's body safe where it is buried in India? I would like to bring him home and have him buried here. Would this be difficult to arrange?'

'He has lain there thirty-five years without being disturbed and I am sure he will remain undisturbed for a long time yet. The grave is not evident to passers-by and it is protected by the car. I suppose someday someone may try to move the car or it may rust away and then the weather may uncover his remains. But I can't think of any reason why anyone would want to undertake the difficult task of moving the rusted wreck. I am sure his remains will remain safe there for a very long time. For bureaucratic reasons, formally exhuming his body and returning it to America is likely to be very difficult.'

'I'd really like to try. The cost is of no concern.'

'As you are aware, the Indian authorities know nothing about this case. To get their cooperation, we would have to provide them with the evidence we have collected. They will then know what we have done without consulting them, and it is unlikely that this will please them. They may then make life very difficult for the forensic people in Mumbai who helped us. I also gave my word to the Indian who was forced to assist in Dan's burial that I would not reveal his identity to anyone. Even if the

Indian authorities don't react negatively, they may still take their time because they will have many more pressing current cases to attend to.'

'I'd still like to try. I have contacts in Washington.'

'I guessed you would want to do this, and I've thought about it a lot since we spoke on the phone. Let me suggest the following approach. I prepare a report summarising the case. I will give a minimum of information and stick to the important facts. Dan Blum disappeared, presumed murdered in India in late 1968. Investigations by Buffalo Investigations and Forensic Inc. into his disappearance began in 1969, but led nowhere. Further information came to hand in 2003 which led to the discovery of his remains in a ravine near Rampur on the Sutlej River in Himalchal Pradesh in India. Evidence at the site has proven conclusively that the killer was an Englishman, Patrick O'Connell alias George Williams. Detective Charoenkul of the Bangkok police can confirm that the bullet which killed Dan Blum came from a Beretta handgun owned by George Williams and discovered at his apartment after he too was murdered. I would hope that the Indian authorities would take such a report at face value, seek details about the location of Dan's body, examine the site, and perhaps somewhat reluctantly acquiesce to the exhumation of his body and allow its return to America. Of course, they will certainly ask further questions, but hopefully none which would cause problems for our colleagues in Mumbai.'

'Would you please do that?'

'I'll have to discuss it first with my boss at Buffalo. I'll let you know as soon as possible.'

'I cannot express in words the extent of my appreciation of what you and Mr and Mrs Webster have done for me. I'd like to invite them to visit me so that I can meet them face-to-face to thank them and hopefully give them the opportunity to discover what New York has to offer. Of course, after their experience of a free holiday in Thailand, they may not wish to accept! But I hope they will. When they come, we can all meet as friends. Would you please give me their mail address so I can write formally to them? Would you also find out the names of their four children?'

'Of course. You should already have the Websters' address. Your friend in Perth gave it to you and you passed it on to Buffalo Investigations! But I'll find out the names of their children.'

'Silly old woman! Yes, I know where the address should be. But if I can't find it, I'll phone you. But please get me their children's names.'

Andy's elderly client stood on tiptoes to plant a kiss on his cheek as he departed.

A week later, in Sydney, Hugh was sitting at his computer catching up with e-mails when he heard the sound of the postman's motorcycle. He went out just in time to meet the mailman at the gate. They exchanged pleasantries about the improved weather and Hugh took charge of a bundle of letters. The only interesting mail was a postcard from one of his brothers travelling in Europe and an airmail letter addressed to Ruth and himself from the USA. It looked important. So he decided not to open it until she returned from their daughter's house.

When Ruth returned an hour later, they opened the letter together. It was quite short.

*Dear Mr and Mrs Webster,*

*We have never met, but you'll know me by name. I'm Esther Blum, and you helped Mr Andy McInnis investigate the disappearance of my son Dan many years ago.*

*I am told you are parents and grandparents. So you will understand the emotions I have experienced over so many years following the mysterious disappearance of my younger son, Dan. Of course, I knew in my heart as the years passed that he was dead. But not knowing what had happened left me without closure. I now know what happened and where and how. It won't bring Dan back, but at least I now have closure.*

*For this I have to thank you and Mr McInnis. You may not really appreciate how much what you have done means to me. If possible, I would very much like to tell you in person. Would you please be kind enough to accept an old lady's offer of a two-week visit to New York so that we can meet and I can arrange for you to see something of 'the Big Apple'?*

*Please say yes! It would make an old lady very happy. It is not possible for me to travel far these days. I know you'll enjoy New York, and I'm sure it won't turn out to be as dangerous as Bangkok!*

*Thank you from the bottom of my heart—and please say yes.*

*Sincerely,*
*Esther Blum*

They immediately wrote back accepting the invitation, and a week later, Andy e-mailed them to make arrangements.

*Hi Ruth and Hugh,*

*I am delighted that you have accepted Mrs Blum's invitation to visit New York and that we will have the opportunity to meet up again (under less-stressful circumstances!) I understand from your acceptance letter too that you have commitments which preclude you coming over here for a couple of months. That's a pity, but the delay will make our reunion even sweeter.*

*I need to get the following information from you:*

1. *the best date for you to leave Sydney;*
2. *whether you would like to spend a few days in Hawaii en route to New York to break the long journey;*
3. *a few things you would definitely like to do in New York (Mrs Blum will then arrange to fill in your days in NY with various tourist activities); and*
4. *the names of your four children (Mrs Blum asked me to find these out).*

*Best regards,*
*Andy*

A large number of important family commitments and some travel talks Hugh had promised to give made the choice of departure date difficult. They also had to think about what they wanted to do in New York. So it was two days before their response e-mail. The other two questions were easy to answer.

Three months later, they were on their way, first class, to New York. They broke the long journey with a three-day stopover in Hawaii before flying directly to Kennedy Airport. Here they were met by a limousine booked by Andy and driven to the Benjamin Hotel on East Fiftieth Street. When they checked in, they were handed an envelope that contained a letter from Mrs Blum, a schedule for their tourist activities and various tickets. Everything was organised and they were very pleased to see that the three things they had requested were included: an evening at the Met, a Broadway production, and a visit to the Guggenheim Museum. The two-week schedule was very full, and they feared that after the two weeks they would have to go home for a rest. They were certainly glad they had broken the long journey for a few days in Honolulu.

Their full program included two meetings with Mrs Blum and Andy, the first a couple of days after their arrival. They found her a charming lady who was clearly delighted that they had accepted her invitation. Before they arrived at her elegant apartment, they wondered whether conversation with her would be difficult. In the event, they found it very easy. She was a sophisticated woman, interested in everything going on in the world. During the evening, she asked a lot about their family and Australia, 'a country, sadly, I have not had the pleasure of visiting'. Apart from thanking the three of them again for what they had done and apologising for the serious situation they had been exposed to in Bangkok, there was no discussion of the case.

The second evening came towards the end of their New York stay. Again the conversation flowed easily. Andy had obviously told her a little about the couple's journey from Cardiff to Bombay and mentioned that they had made another major journey more recently in their own car from Malaysia to London. Much of that evening was spent talking about these adventures and the countries they had visited. Ruth and Hugh had brought an autographed copy of their book about these journeys with them, and shortly before they said farewell, they gave it to her. Mrs Blum reciprocated by handing them five very smart envelopes. The top one was simply addressed 'Mr and Mrs Webster' in elegant handwriting.

'Please don't open it now.'

She said the same to Andy when she gave him a similar envelope.

When they got back to their room at the Benjamin, the Australians opened their envelope. It contained a card with a lovely message from Mrs Blum in beautiful handwriting.

> *Dear Mr and Mrs Webster,*
>     *I have already told you how much I appreciate all that you have done for me. The gift attached is a token of this appreciation.*
>     *You are blessed with four children of whom you are very proud. You are very fortunate. The other envelopes contain gifts for them.*
>
> *Sincerely,*
> *Esther Blum*

The gift attached to the letter was a cheque for $20,000. They were staggered.

'Yes. We are blessed.'

'We don't really need the money. Perhaps we should give some or all of this to assist others who are not as fortunate.'

Andy telephoned them the morning of their flight back to Sydney. They both spoke with him and chatted as close friends. They hoped it would not be too long before they meet up again somewhere. Hugh asked whether the Barbies Bar owner had been convicted and sentenced. They were surprised and very concerned by what he told them. Robinson had been convicted of corruption and sentenced to five years' jail, although he was appealing the judgement. Three police officers had received similar sentences. Although he was charged with soliciting the kidnap and murder of Hugh, Ruth, and Andy, the court deemed that the evidence provided was insufficient and he was not convicted. A charge of murder in relation to George Williams was also thrown out of court for the same reason. The thought of Robinson being free in five years' time was worrying. They hoped that on his release, he would not try to seek vengeance. If he did, then hopefully his criminal record would prevent him getting a visa into Australia.

Two days later, they were back home. Their children were amazed by the cheques they received from Mrs Blum. Their son Peter showed his parents the message from Mrs Blum.

*Dear Peter,*

*You have probably learned from your parents how they helped solve the mystery of my son Dan's disappearance many years ago. Sadly, I have lost both of my children.*

*Your parents are very blessed to have all their children and you are fortunate to have such wonderful parents.*

*Please accept this gift, which I want you to have in recognition of what your parents have done for me.*

*Sincerely,*
*Esther Blum*

The cheque was for $5,000.

# Synopsis

When a young American draft dodger from the Vietnam War disappears, his anxious parents seek the help of a Buffalo NY investigation company. The last coded postcard they received from their son indicated that he was hiding out in Afghanistan. The investigator photographs two bearded American young men camped in Kabul arguing with a better-dressed Englishman, but neither is the missing son. The trail goes cold.

Thirty-five years later, a Western Australian friend of the widowed mother uncovers the names of an Australian couple who were camped in Kabul at the time and might be able to provide clues to the young man's disappearance. The search is renewed, taking the investigators to Pakistan, the Indian Himalayas, the red-light area of Bangkok, and to neighbouring Laos.

Printed in Australia
AUOC02n0713200214
259901AU00002B/4/P

9 781493 105731